Hunted Mate

Hunted Mate

Kari Thomas

Black Lyon Publishing, LLC

HUNTED MATE
Copyright © 2008 by KARI THOMAS

Our books may be ordered through your local bookstore or by visiting the publisher:

www.BlackLyonPublishing.com

Black Lyon Publishing, LLC
PO Box 567
Baker City, OR 97814

This is a work of fiction. All of the characters, names, events, organizations and conversations in this novel are either the products of the author's vivid imagination or are used in a fictitious way for the purposes of this story.

ISBN-10:   1-934912-03-4
ISBN-13:   978-1-934912-03-4
Library of Congress Control Number: 2008924463

Cover Model: Sean C. Rea

Written, published and printed in
the United States of America.

Black Lyon Paranormal Romance

To my dad for being as proud of this
second book as he was the first one.
And to my dear friend, Mary Corrales,
for insisting that this story needed to
be a full-length adventure.

Chapter One

I owe you a life debt, Damian. And if this is what it takes to repay that debt, then I have no other choice.

His earlier declaration echoed in his thoughts as Logan Cross left his downtown office of Lnx, Inc. and drove out of Spokane toward the Interstate. He'd left Luke in charge of everything until he returned; his younger brother was capable of handling anything thrown his way and Logan didn't worry. If something serious popped up, the Council would step in to help.

He grimaced. His Council hadn't been happy about his decision to agree to this mission. They warned it was too dangerous, and could very well turn out to be a trap. Logan had to admit he'd been suspicious when Damian had sent word that he wanted to talk to him. The Shifter Cat Prince and the Wolf Prince hadn't seen each other since that fateful day twenty years back.

That day had put Logan in debt to Damian.

But Logan Cross was a man of his word and he would repay that debt no matter the cost. He didn't have to like the conditions, but he wasn't going to back down now.

Awhile later Logan drove past the entrance to Riverside State Park, and his thoughts went back to yesterday and the meeting with Damian.

It had been late evening when he'd arrived at the Park. He'd left his car in the parking lot and jogged into the darkening interior of the forest. There was less chance that a human would be wandering around that far into the wooded area this time of night. Most of the campers and hikers would be settling in for the night in the restricted areas of the Park.

Once he assessed he was far enough into the woods, Logan shifted into his cat form. His natural shape shifting ability made the transaction easy and quick. With just a fleeting thought he willed his clothes to disappear. He stretched for a moment, enjoying the feeling of cool air caressing over his naked body. His tanned skin began to stretch tighter, become darker. His bones and muscles re-shaped. Soft, short cat fur grew over his body as he smoothly morphed into his cat counterpart. Moments later, the thirty-year-old man he'd been was now replaced with a full-grown shifter cat.

Anyone spotting the large mountain lion would assume it had wandered in from the mountains to prowl the Park's forested confinement. Seven feet in length, from his large head to his long tail, the big cat was an impressive body of toned muscles and sleek golden fur.

Logan's eyes perused the area around him, noting even the slightest movement of nature or animal. The serene atmosphere of the majestic park was like a calming balm to his volatile emotions. Damian's imperious summons had him angry that he'd had no choice but to obey them.

The evening air from the nearby mountains was cool, flowing through the tall trees, and down onto him. The evening's descending darkness whispered seductively to his primal animal nature, beckoning him further into the concealing woods. He lifted his head and sniffed the air to take in the varied scents. He was assured that there were no humans around.

He glided on padded paws further into the forest's interior. Yards in, his acute sense of smell caught the scent of an animal near. He recognized the musky scent of the wolf shifter, and his feline lips curled in a snarl of distaste. The shifter was hiding behind a boulder about ten feet away from him, careful to stay hidden. Logan swallowed his automatic growling reaction. Was the wolf foolish enough to try and ambush him?

Although they tolerated each other's presence in the Washington State area, the Wolf and Cat Shifter Clans were natural enemies. They avoided each other in the animal world and in their human environment, too. As it was, an uneasy truce existed only because their Princes demanded it. It was the only way to keep a shifter war from breaking out and spilling into the human world.

Logan shook his furry head. Not for the first time today he wondered why he had agreed to this meeting.

Because he owed Damian his life.

And he was honor-bound to repay that debt—even if it meant agreeing to the enemy's condition of repayment. *Whatever he demands of me.*

It was time to get it over with. He didn't like being in wolf territory, especially not knowing what to expect. Logan preferred going into any situation prepared. He was rarely caught off guard with anything or anyone because he was as ruthless in his animal habitat as he was in his business world. Still, he couldn't get rid of this gut instinct that the sooner this was over with then the better for all concerned. The uneasy feeling kept him tense, overly alert, and ready to fight at any moment. Hell, he'd been in a fighting mood since receiving the summons from Damian!

Using the telepathic path that all shifters communicated on while in animal form, Logan acknowledged the hiding shifter, "I don't have time for this hide and seek game, so you can come out now."

A dark brown wolf glided from around the boulder and faced Logan. His short, coarse fur stood straight on end, bristling down his back. Posture stiff, he braced his four legs in an obvious fighting stance, and his ears went flat against his head. His lips pulled back in a snarl and he growled low. "It took you long enough to get here. Damian doesn't like to be kept waiting."

Logan resisted the urge to teach the arrogant pup a lesson in manners. His lion's body was larger than the wolf's, and he was a far more seasoned fighter. One or two swipes of his large, razor sharp claws and the measly dog would go down. Luck was on the wolf's side though, because Logan didn't have the time to spare. And, starting a fight with the wolf shifter wasn't the best way to show he was ready to pay the debt he owed to the Wolf Clan's Prince.

Putting just enough snarl into his tone to show the wolf he wouldn't tolerate his attitude, Logan commanded, "Lead the way, pup. Let's not keep your Prince waiting."

The wolf snarled in defiance, but was smart enough not to push his luck. He turned away and trotted off. Preternatural senses on full alert, Logan followed. Willingly going into the heart of wolf shifter territory wasn't the smartest thing he'd ever done, but he didn't have a choice. Damian Sinclair had become a recluse since his claim to the Pack's leadership and he seldom ventured back into the world of humans. He'd requested that Logan meet him in the privacy of the shifter world rather than among humans.

Walking straight into the wolf pack's den in his lion's form had Logan doubting his sanity for the hundredth time since the summons had come. Not for the first time, he wondered why Damian had chosen now, after all these years, to seek repayment of the life debt. His Clan had repeatedly warned Logan it might be a trap. For months now, territorial claims and enemy-based fights were a daily occurrence between the cat and wolf clans. Damian's iron willed control over the Wolf Pack that called Washington State home, had managed to keep things a little more civilized between the two dominant shifter clans. Yet they all knew that the uneasy truce between the shifters wasn't meant to be a permanent solution. Logan knew it was just a matter of time after he fulfilled his oath to Damian that the battle lines would be drawn again.

Change was coming; he could feel it. All the species of shifters were more restless, more aggressive. The Cat Council had debated on the reasons behind the volatile dissension and had concluded it might have something to do with the Prophecy of the Shifter Goddess Azina. It had been predicted for centuries that the time for the Fulfillment would come in the early twenty-first century.

Unfortunately for all shifters concerned, the records of the Prophecy had been lost and no one alive knew the exact predictions anymore. Rumors circulated that one species of shifters would be chosen to rule over all the others in the world. Other predictions claimed that Goddess Azina would choose an army of shifters from among all the different species and they would rule over the shifter world. Very few of the shifters, in any species, were happy with the assumptions. But all anyone could do was—wait.

And Logan hated waiting. It just wasn't in his nature, despite being cat. He'd got where he was by being aggressive and making things happen when he wanted them to. He was Prince of the Cat Clans by birthright, and he controlled every shifter-owned business in the Washington State area. His Council took care of the international businesses the Cat Clans owned around the world.

Always the one in complete control, Logan wasn't happy about being led like a sheep to the slaughter now, especially on the decree of a wolf. If his Council had any more say in the matter, they would have locked him up for safekeeping. It wouldn't have worked; he'd laugh at their attempts and do as he wanted anyway.

Logan pushed away his uneasy musings and concentrated on his surroundings as he followed the wolf deeper into the forest. He was still surrounded by the feel of serenity in the park's interior, but the deeper in they traveled, the more he started to sense the changing of the atmosphere. There were less wild animals roaming around here than in other areas of the park. He knew the Pack that chose to stay with Damian in the wilds wasn't very big, but they had to travel further for hunting grounds as the park became inundated with campers and hikers each season.

Why do they stay and live like this instead of blending with the rest of the world? It was a mystery he figured he'd never understand. Like all shifters, he was proud of his heritage and gloried in the abilities he had been born with. But he also preferred living in the human world with all the amenities it offered, too.

The heavy-treed forest thinned out to open into a small clearing by a stream. The wolf trotted forward and stopped to drink at the stream before jumping over it. He turned and looked at Logan, his wolf eyes glinting with arrogance. Logan had already scented the sentry guards, wolf shifters, who now circled him from their concealment in the nearby bushes. He didn't like the caged-in feeling, surrounded by the six shifter guards, but he managed to stifle his urge to stand and fight. He had to trust Damian's word that this was a meeting, only, and not a trap.

Logan jumped the creek and then glided into the small clearing with his head high, his tail twitching in warning, and his eyes narrowed. Wolves of all colors and sizes stood at a discreet distance around the perimeter of the clearing, and in its center sat a huge grey wolf. Damian's pack was larger than he'd expected. If he had to fight his way out of here, Logan didn't think he stood much of a chance at getting out alive.

He stopped a few feet from the grey wolf and acknowledged him with a slight bowing of his head. He managed to keep the aggression out of his tone. "It's been a long time, Damian."

The grey wolf nodded his head, the simple action regal. "Thank you for coming, Logan. I'm sure you realize I would not have asked this of you had there been any other option." He turned his head and surveyed the wolves surrounding them. "Leave us to our privacy."

A large black wolf, one of the sentry guards, snarled in protest. "We do not feel right in leaving you alone with the lion, Prince Damian."

Damian's canine lips curled up, exposing large white teeth. He stared at the other wolf who quickly bowed his head in submission. "You doubt my ability to protect myself should the need arise? Your insult will be addressed later, Bren. Go now. All of you."

As one, every wolf lowered their eyes and bowed their heads in respect to his command and obediently slinked away into the surrounding forest. Logan sniffed the air and noted the musky dog scents slowly faded as the pack disappeared from sight.

To Logan's surprise, Damian's entire body suddenly slumped and he sat back on his heels. The two Princes stared at each other for long moments. Looking closer, Logan noted that Damian's natural grey coat lacked the normal lustrous sheen wolf shifters had. Damian looked aged. Logan wasn't sure how old the wolf was, though he knew for a fact he'd been Prince for decades. Shifters weren't immortal but they did live longer than humans, so there wasn't a way to guess at Damian's exact age.

Logan broke the strained silence. "What's going on, Damian? Why have you called me here?"

Damian sighed and even that soft sound was tired. Logan's unease increased. "I never thought to hold you to the life-debt, Logan. I saved your life that fateful day because it was the right thing to do." His dark grey eyes snared Logan's gaze, glowing oddly. "But I have need of your help now. I've been out of touch with the human world for a long time, so you will know better than I if the rumors are true."

"Rumors?" Logan sat back on his haunches. "If you're referring to the Prophecy talk, I've heard, but it's nothing new, Damian. If you mean the increase in territorial fights among our Clans, then yes, that's true." Logan shrugged his shoulders. "It was bound to happen sooner or later. Washington isn't big enough for both our Clans."

Damian chuckled, the sound raspy in his canine throat. "Spoken like a true warrior prince. Your reputation is well known, Logan. You don't give an inch, in any situation."

Logan frowned. It was true he had a reputation as one of the most aggressive and dangerous members of the Cat Clans, in business and in shifter life, but he dealt with situations with complete integrity. It was that same strict sense of moral that had him here now to repay a debt.

"Get to the point, Damian. Why did you call me here? You know

I am willing to repay my debt to you. And then we need not ever meet again."

Damian nodded his head in acknowledgment of the statement. "I need you to fetch something for me, Logan. It's so valuable I can't trust any other shifter with this." He exhaled a deep sigh before continuing in a low, tired tone, "I can't even trust one of my own."

Logan straightened from his relaxed crouch. He didn't like the implications of this. "Why not a wolf shifter? What the hell is so important that you can't trust one of your own clan members with it?"

"It's a *she*, Logan." Damian paused long, to let the words sink in. "And she is my mate."

Logan choked back his surprised exclamation. Did he just hear right? Of all the requests he'd expected from Damian this sure as hell wasn't one of them! He shook his furry head, his ears twitching in aggravation.

"Mate? What are you talking about, Damian? Hell, I think old age is starting to affect your mind." He stood on all fours and started pacing, his cat instincts rearing to life. It was time to get this resolved and get out of here. "You're asking me to fetch your mate? I'm not a carrier, Damian, and I'm not a wolf. Send one of your own to fetch her. Or better yet, fetch her yourself." He snarled. "Damn. I can't believe this is what you ask in repayment of my debt to you."

Damian sighed again, the heavy sound loud and rough. "I can't trust anyone else, Logan. Calm down and let me explain. If you still refuse to do this after I tell you everything, then so be it. Her name is Tara Stuart. She lives in a small town just north of the Great Salt Lake in Utah. And she's human, Logan."

Logan spit out a round of swear words before he managed to get control of his anger. "Hell and damnation!" He couldn't believe what he was hearing. "Tell me you're joking. You just said she was your mate. How is it possible that she could be human? Is she a half-breed?"

"She doesn't have a drop of shifter blood in her," Damian replied. "But she's not fully human either. She's a direct descendent of the Shifter Goddess Azina."

Logan muttered under his breath. He didn't bother disguising the sarcasm in his tone. "Now I know you're crazy. You are trying to claim a human woman—who has Goddess blood in her veins, albeit eons diluted—as your mate?"

"Yes." Damian met Logan's hard glare without blinking, a glint of challenge in his eyes.

Logan's eyes narrowed. He didn't like the sound of any of this; it sounded simple enough but he was suspicious of the wolf's motives. "You're not telling me the full story."

The old wolf acknowledged the truth with a nod of his head and another tired sigh. "You're right. Goddess Azina's Prophecy has an addendum that concerns the wolf clans. When the time comes, one of the reigning wolf princes will claim one of Her descendents as his mate. When that union is complete, the Goddess powers she will inherit will also become his. Together they will have the complete power to reign over the entire world of wolf clans.

"I was told by the Clan Seer that I am the predicted wolf prince. And that Tara Stuart is to be my chosen mate.

"But there's an obstacle standing in the way of this prophesized union, Logan. There are dissenters among the wolf clans who believe I'm not the chosen prince. Others are claiming that right. They want Tara's goddess powers for their own means.

"They have been searching for her for centuries, waiting for the woman to be born that bears the mark of the Shifter Goddess. The main reason she has been safe from those wanting to claim her for the past twenty years of her life is that the mark isn't on a noticeable spot of her body. It's in the palm of her left hand.

"One of my pack members was in her area and spotted the mark on her, recognizing it immediately. It was an unexpected miracle."

A miracle? Logan didn't like the implications. "Are you saying that if the mark had not been spotted, you wouldn't have known who she was or where she was? Damn, Damian. This is crazy!" He hissed under his breath.

"It was necessary to protect her identity. Even from the wolf clans. *Especially* the wolf clans," Damian answered.

Logan scratched his ear trying to look as if this wasn't something that had loud warning bells going off in his head. He wondered what his Cat Council would have to say about this new bit of information concerning the Goddess's Prophecy. What did this mean for the other shifter species if the wolf clans were the only ones chosen to be united with the Goddess's descendents?

War would break out. There wouldn't be any way around it. The different species of shifters in the world would never willingly unite under one clan's rule. Hell, even he would fight to keep his clans from being subjugated to a wolf's rule.

Logan stared hard at Damian. "So, what's stopping you from claiming this Stuart woman? Other than the fact she's human and will obviously think you're a nut case when you tell her this crazy story."

"I can't leave here," Damian answered, his tone sounding even more tired. Logan glanced sharply at him, once again noticing how aged he was looking. The mental warning bells in his head got louder.

"I'm needed here. To keep things under control. Events have been happening that I can't go into detail about right now, but suffice to say that if I were to suddenly leave on a journey then chances are my Clan wouldn't survive. And too, I can't take the chance I'll be followed and lead the others who are searching for Tara straight to her. If they got to her first, Logan ..."

Logan's fur stood on end, the warning bells pounding inside his head like a hammer-wielding mantra, demanding that he leave now, before things got even more complicated. "If what?" he demanded. "Don't drag this out, Damian."

"Tara's goddess powers will only come into being after she's mated," Damian explained. "If another wolf gets to her first and claims her, he can also claim her powers. Until she's safely mated to me then she is free game to any wolf shifter out there. With me, her life and comfort will be first priority. With another wolf ... there's no telling. Her very life could be forfeit once her powers are shared. Her goddess powers are a heady temptation, Logan, for any shifter. If those powers are wielded by the wrong person ..."

Then all hell would break loose. Between the wolf clans. And among every shifter clan the world over. With that kind of power in the wrong hands there was no telling what could happen.

Logan cursed. "Damn. What a nightmare that could turn out to be."

Damian nodded his head. "They are searching for her now. Once the rumor got out that she had been spotted, her life was at stake."

He had no choice and Logan knew it. If Damian couldn't leave to bring Tara back here then that left one other man who could guarantee her safety. Logan had never backed down from a challenge in his life. He wasn't about to do so now. He owed Damian, and if this was the only way to repay him, then he would do it. He didn't have to like it, and he would worry about the consequences of bringing a goddess mate to a wolf shifter—later.

"Any ideas on how I'm supposed to accomplish this crazy mission?" he demanded. "For some reason, I don't think telling Tara that I have to bring her here to become the mate to a shifter wolf so they can both obtain goddess powers, has that much going for it. She'll run as fast and as far as she can to escape the lunatic she'll believe me to be."

"There's more," Damian said. He had the decency to look guilty.

"Spit it out," Logan growled, "before I have to kill you, and start a war."

Damian's reply was a soft chuckle. But then he sobered as he answered, "Because she bears the goddess mark meant to indicate she is to mate with a wolf shifter, she will be like a beacon to any wolf shifter out there that gets wind of her. They'll be drawn to her and there's no way to prevent that. They'll all be looking for her, searching harder now, and most likely in packs. Chances are that you will have to fight off every wolf shifter you come across before you get her back here. It won't be an easy task. I'm sorry, Logan."

Logan sighed, the sound coming from deep within him. Yet, he straightened to his full height and lifted his head. He'd repay this debt, no matter the cost. He could only hope that in doing so, it wasn't the biggest mistake of his life. His gut instinct was telling him that it just might turn out that way.

"I owe you a life-debt, Damian. And if this is what it takes to repay that debt, then I have no other choice."

He'd bring Tara Stuart, a.k.a. goddess-to-be, back to Damian if it was the last thing he ever did.

No matter the cost.

Chapter Two

She had a split-second to wrestle the car's steering wheel to the left and stomp her foot down on the brakes, bringing the car to a skidding halt. As it was, she still wasn't sure she'd managed to avoid hitting the small dog that had dashed out in front of her car. She'd heard the little bump as she'd swerved the car.

Tara Stuart gulped in a huge shaky breath and then let it out in the same shaky exhale, dropping her forehead onto the steering wheel. Oh, Goddess! She'd never forgive herself if she had hit the poor animal! She should have been paying attention to her driving instead of being preoccupied with the dire thoughts of this morning's events.

Trembling and feeling sick to her stomach, she got out of the car and looked around. She perused both ways down the highway. At this time of evening the old, two-lane road back into town was almost deserted. It ran through a long stretch of farmlands and homesteads before leading into the small, drive-through town of Grant, Utah. Countless acres of farmland stretched for miles on either side of the road where she now stood.

"Come here, puppy," she called out softly, not wanting to scare the poor animal any more than it was. She walked around the car and then got down on her hands and knees to look underneath it. Where had the little animal run off to? Was he hurt? Maybe he had run into the ditch area beside the road?

"Come on, puppy, don't hide."

Tara crossed the road and searched the steep incline of the ditch. She couldn't see anything moving but it didn't mean the little animal wasn't there. The ditch was wide, full of mud, water, and vegetation— and it was possible the little dog had fallen into the water and not been able to surface.

Resigned, she sighed. There was only one way to find out and that was to go down there. She took a few cautious steps and started down the steep incline of the irrigation ditch. She should have known better than to try this, wearing high heels no less, but then again she hadn't been thinking straight all day. Before she could even finish the squeal of "Oh no!" she lost her footing on the slippery slope and was falling forward. Straight down into the ditch.

She landed with a loud splat. Into the knee-deep muddy water. Face first.

Sputtering and spitting out a mouthful of foul muddy water, Tara clumsily got back to her feet. Thank the Goddess the ditch was only knee deep. Mud and ditch debris sloshed off her in slow motion. She groaned and glanced skyward. "This just didn't happen," she muttered, wiping the mud out of her eyes and mouth. "Not after the day I've had. The Fates wouldn't be so cruel."

Oh yes they would. Wasn't today proof enough? Disgusted, and now past the point of caring, she climbed up the embankment. Slipping and sliding, getting muddier, and grumbling every inch of the climb, she made her way back to the edge of the road. *Who told the Fates what I had planned, anyway? It just figures that someone was a tattletale.*

Tara sat down with an ungraceful plop onto the ground by the side of her car. Her mud-caked clothes made a disgusting squishy sound and she grimaced. She didn't know whether to laugh or cry. She knew she looked like one messy lump of mud and clay, from head to toes. Resigned and feeling defeated, she mentally grumbled that this day was the worst she'd had since ...

She stopped that trail of thoughts immediately. She didn't want to go there. Today's events were a direct result of that fateful day, and she didn't want to have to think about it. Not yet. All she was going to allow herself to think about was getting home. Getting a nice warm bath. And going to bed. *I'll be like Scarlet O'Hara and think about it tomorrow.*

A slight rustle in the bush near the back of the car made her remember the dog she might have hit. The mud was slowly drying in the most uncomfortable way and it made her movements clumsy as she stood up. She walked to the back of the car and then approached the bush.

"Are you there, puppy?" She grimaced as the bush shook in answer. Under her breath she mumbled, "The way my luck has been lately, I'm about to face a skunk instead of a dog."

The thought made her hesitate. But she swallowed down her trepidation and pushed the limbs of the bush aside.

She came face to face with the biggest house cat she had ever seen. Yellow, from what she could tell of its matted, muddied fur, and looking like the most forlorn animal in the world. The cat looked up at her and uttered a pitiful meow, then held up its injured paw.

"Oh, kitty. I did hit you. I'm so sorry." Careful of the bleeding paw, Tara reached down and gathered the cat into her arms. She almost fell again. "Whoa. Despite your half-starved look, you are really heavy. Must be all that muscle under this matted fur."

Surprised that the cat would meekly allow her to pick him up, Tara carried it back to her car. Each step she took made her uncomfortably aware of her mud caked clothes sticking to her every inch. Her high heels were covered in caked mud and made loud plopping sounds as she walked.

Ignoring the embarrassing noises, she spoke in a low tone to the cat, "You probably belong to one of the farms around here, don't you?" She glanced both ways down the deserted road. "But there are too many to check, and it's getting late." She'd take the cat home, nurse its injured paw, and then try to find the owner tomorrow. It would give her something else to concentrate on for awhile instead of today's fateful events.

She grimaced at her and the cat's muddy bodies as she chewed on her bottom lip. Was all the mud in the world stuck to them? She shook her head and opened the door to her soft-leathered upholstery sports car. Careful not to cause him anymore discomfort she deposited the cat onto the seat of the passenger side. He just sat there, not even bothering to try and get out. She walked around the car and then grimaced again as she slid onto the driver's seat and the mud made a splat as it dropped off her in wet chunks to fall to the floor. She closed the door and then looked over at the cat who sat staring straight at her.

"Aren't we a pair." She wiped the mud off her hands before starting the car. "But I have a feeling I'm more of a mess than you."

As if to prove her wrong the cat meowed pitifully and raised its injured paw.

She grinned. "Okay, kitty. Point taken. Let's go home."

Ten minutes later Tara drove up to the gated entrance of the small, yet out-of-place-for-the-area estate. With a flick of the remote control on her dashboard, she closed the gates behind her and drove up the long, winding driveway to the garage of the house.

Resembling an old fashioned manor home from the days of the Old South, the three story house was pristine white and noticeably elegant. The mayor of the town had once lived there, but Tara's family bought the estate when he decided he wanted to move into something smaller with less grandeur. Fifteen acres of overgrown orchards surrounded the house on all four sides, and was left unfarmed since her family didn't care to use the property for profit. Gated and fenced, the rest of the estate was surrounded by miles and miles of more country acres. It was perfect for the needed privacy and seclusion the Stuart family sought.

Tara stared at the manor as she drove the car into the garage. It was bad enough that the town thought of them as eccentric, out-of-place foreigners. She hated to think what it would be like if the ninety-nine percent religious residents of Grant knew the full truth about her family.

They had chosen Utah for its religious-based communities, with the idea that not too many people would think them strange to claim it was their own personal religion that would keep them reclusive. With an average of two hundred citizens in the small town, it wasn't unusual that everyone knew about the Stuarts. It was known that they were from Scotland, a family of five with two grown daughters and a younger son. Tara was the middle child. Their parents, Colleen and Lach, were reclusive artists and seldom ventured away from the estate. Tara knew that rumors were constantly active about what the three children did as careers since they were seldom seen around town that much either.

If the truth were known ...

She parked her car next to her brother's jeep and got out. She opened the passenger side car door and leaned in to scoop the cat up into her arms. She gave a mock "oomph" about his weight and then cuddled him close. She looked down at the pitiful animal and muttered, "Don't be surprised if they throw us back out, and straight into the pool. Dragging all this mud into Mother's pristine, spotless home isn't the best idea I've had all day."

The cat meowed as if in understanding.

She chose the shortest route from the garage, through the kitchen, and up the wide stairs to her third floor bedroom. With every step she took, dried mud flaked off and left a trail behind her. Once inside her suite she took the cat straight to the adjoining bathroom and sat him down on the marble counter by the sink.

"Okay, kitty, let's see how bad you're hurt."

She cleaned his large paw with a wet cloth, careful not to hurt him more. He sat meekly, watching her. She was glad to see there wasn't much blood, and the cut appeared to be smaller than she had first thought.

"I must not have hit you with the car after all. This cut is too small and looks as though it's a few days old. It must have started bleeding again when you raced across the road."

Tara smiled. She realized she was talking to the cat as if he understood her every word. Surprisingly, she thought he did appear to be concentrating on every thing she said as his large blue eyes stayed locked with her own gaze. After putting a dab of antiseptic on the cut, she continued to talk to him in soothing tones as she ran the wet cloth over his muddied body to clean him, "Mother will have a fit if she finds you in the house. Cats belong with witches, not goddesses. That's what she always said when I'd ask for one. I should have known when she let Jason have that wolf as a pet that it meant she just didn't like cats."

She gave him a gentle pat on his large head and grinned. "Don't worry, though. She wouldn't turn a poor wounded kitten out into the cold." She laughed softly when he blinked rapidly several times as if questioning her statement. "Okay, so it's not cold out there and you're not exactly a kitten are you? I'm guessing you must weigh at least twenty pounds."

"Tara!" A loud, indignant voice shouted from the hallway, "You're in soooo much trouble!"

Tara jumped and swung towards the voice. The cat stiffened, fur bristling, and he growled menacingly.

"Stop that, kit," she hushed with a gentle rebuke. "Let's not make the situation worse by you attacking one of my family members." Things were bad enough right now without adding any more complications.

A striking, lovely, blonde woman entered the bathroom. She was taller than Tara, slim and elegant. Her blonde hair was darker than Tara's golden streaks and longer past her slim shoulders. Her eyes were a dark blue and sparkled with an inner fire that always made her gaze appear mysterious. Tara often thought of her as a mini-volcano ready to erupt at the least provocation. She bit back a groan. *And this looks like one of those times.*

Hands on hips, the woman glared at Tara then pointedly stared at the cat. "What the hell is that?"

Tara stepped protectively in between the cat on the counter and her sister. "Stop cursing, Mara. And it's a cat, of course. I almost hit it with my car."

Mara Stuart stared hard at her younger sister. "Okay, I can tell that's a cat. But I'm not really sure you're my sister. Why are you looking like a mud-mummy? You left a mud-print trail all the way from the garage. Mother and Father are already upset about your trip, and then you come home looking like this. Are you just asking for more problems?"

Tara sighed. The cat growled again. Mara glared at them both.

Her sister was right. Things were about to get worse. "I'll clean up and then be downstairs to talk to them," she said. She glanced back at the cat as he growled again at her sister. "And, Mara, don't mention the cat. You know how Mother is about them."

She was dreading having to tell them the news. She had done the unthinkable and disobeyed the Prophecy. Colleen and Lach's rebellious middle child had caused a problem that wasn't going to be so easy to forgive. But she had done the only thing she could think to do. *This is my life, and I won't let that ancient prophecy ruin it!*

The rebellious thought sounded a lot braver mentally than when said aloud. She sighed, her heart heavy.

After Mara left, Tara carried the cat into her bedroom and deposited it in the middle of her huge canopy bed. "Rest here while I take a bath."

She looked down at her mud covered body and grimaced. She hated being the least bit dirty, and right now she was an absolute mess. Careful not to make more of a mess on her pristine white carpet, she slowly peeled off her mud-stiff clothes as she headed back to the bathroom. Even after leaving a trail of mud-caked clothes behind her, her body was still just as mud covered when she stepped into the glass enclosed shower and under the rain stream shower head. She turned it to full force.

Her sigh was weary and bone deep. *If only I could wash away the problems as easy as this water does the mud ...*

•

He knew he should just stay where she'd put him, but Logan's wayward thoughts had tortured him long enough while the shower ran, and he tried to be patient for her to come back into the room. When she'd started pulling off her clothes as she walked to the bathroom, he had swallowed back so many appreciative growls for the curvy form revealed under all that mud that he thought he'd explode. He couldn't wait to see what the clean Tara—without clothes—looked like. He wasn't even sure of her hair color.

But, oh man, those eyes. Startling periwinkle, large and long lashed; he'd never seen any more beautiful. He'd looked deep into those remarkable eyes when she'd first picked him up and had felt like he was drowning, oh-so-willingly, in a sea of blue and purple flowers. *Great. Now I'm sounding like a love-sick poet!* He shook his furry head in disgust and jumped down off the bed.

A slight twinge of pain from his injured paw forced him to remember why he was here. He'd actually cut the paw with his own claw so he would appear injured when she stopped the car. He'd purposely run out in front of her car, careful not to be hit, and streaked across the road. Tumbling down into the muddied ditch had been an accident. He hadn't realized he was that close to the ditch until too late.

Logan smiled. If he hadn't been in cat form then, he would have laughed his head off when Tara went sliding down that slope and straight into the ditch face first. The comical sight of her flailing her arms, scrambling to get her high heels into a firm grasp of ground, and then landing first on her butt only to topple head over heels into the ditch, was a memory he'd keep forever.

Any other woman would have had a screaming fit. He had to admit his admiration for her grew instantly in that moment. Tara Stuart pulled herself to her feet, wiped the mud from her mouth and eyes and then muttered something about the cruelty of the Fates.

Then, despite her uncomfortable predicament, she had searched for the injured animal without another complaint falling from her lips. Despite not wanting to be, Logan had been very impressed, his opinion of her rising another favorable notch.

He had discreetly studied her for weeks now, learning her habits, her temperament, her personality, and adding everything to his mental list while he tried to figure out the best way to approach her. He had the feeling that walking up to her and announcing he was there to take her to the leader of a shifter wolf clan wasn't going to work well.

How much did she know of her destiny? Despite learning all he could about her, he still wasn't sure just how much she knew about the Prophecy. Her acquaintances were all full humans, as far as he could tell. She lived a normal life, a young artist just coming out in her career. She seldom left her home and family, and then it was only to attend art shows, or visit with a few human friends in the Salt Lake area. Her latest visit to Salt Lake City had lasted longer than the previous ones. Logan hadn't been happy with what he'd discovered there.

He'd deal with that later. Right now he had to decide when the best time was to reveal his true identity. Very few people knew of the existence of shapeshifters. Like vampires, werewolves, witches and sorcerers, ghoulies-and-ghosties-and-things-that-go-bump-in-the-night, and all other supernatural beings, shapeshifters were thought of as just another myth. Even though many shapeshifters and other supernatural beings worked side by side in the world with humans, they were careful to keep their associations with the humans to a minimal in order to keep their secrets safe. Logan's own companies employed only shifters because of the danger of discovery.

And here he was in a tiny, out of the way, farm town in Utah about to expose himself as a shapeshifter to a woman who may or may not know they even existed. *Hell. This isn't going to be easy.* But he'd known that, all along. A debt was a debt, no matter the conditions; he was determined to clear his as soon as possible.

He heard the shower turn off. The shifter in him knew he had a job to do, but the male in him wasn't thinking about the job. Just the woman.

All-human, primal male instinct was the stronger influence at the moment. He didn't bother trying to reason out why his human side was fighting against his cat nature right then. Warning bells should be going off telling him to be careful exposing his secret. Instead, conflicting emotions were bombarding his cat's natural self-preservation, and he didn't bother to fight them.

With a mock-casual meow, he announced himself as he sauntered into the bathroom just as she was stepping out of the shower.

He was in mid-jump to the counter when he turned his head to look at her.

Logan lost his breath, his thoughts, and his balance. Feet flailing in nothing but space, he made a last moment's attempt to reach the counter … and missed by inches. He hit the floor with a loud, painful thump.

He mentally cussed a blue streak; words that would have shocked Tara beyond belief had she heard them. He didn't know whether it was embarrassment or anger that seared his gut as he glared up at the object of his sole, rapt attention.

A naked Tara.

Oh, man. He was almost glad he wasn't in human form at that moment. His human body's automatic, hot-blooded, male reaction would have been hard to hide.

"Oh, kit! What are you doing? Do you want to hurt yourself again?" A naked Tara rushed forward and scooped him up into her arms and cuddled him close to her wet body. Logan didn't know whether to cuss again, or to purr. As it was, he was sure his ragged groan came out sounding a bit too human.

Tara sat him down on the counter and turned away to grab a towel. Inner wisdom and a touch of remaining decency told him to close his eyes and not look at her.

He lost the mental battle.

She was absolute perfection. His intent, hungry gaze roamed over every beautiful inch of her naked body. Rosy-tinted skin glistened wet from her shower over a body that would instantly set any man's libido on fire. She had curves in all the right places. Her breasts were small yet perfectly rounded with erect, rose-tinted nipples. Her stomach was flat, and her waist curvy. Her hips were slim.

Logan perused the silky length of her long legs, all the way to her slender, tiny feet. Those sexy-shaped legs gave him thoughts he knew he shouldn't be thinking. It didn't take any effort to visualize those legs wrapped tight around his waist and back as he …

He jerked his gaze upward and immediately halted that dangerous trail of thoughts. Unfortunately for his peace of mind his line of vision then centered exclusively on the area of soft, bare skin that covered her feminine mound. The area was smooth and silky; she waxed there. Why the knowledge was so hot and erotic, he wasn't sure because he just couldn't manage to think straight.

His mouth watered. His body temperature went up several more notches. He couldn't help it; his mind was awash with mental images so X-rated he was actually disgusted with himself.

Dammit!

He shook his head, trying valiantly to dispel the thoughts and images. He forced out a meow just to remind himself where he was and in what form.

What am I thinking, letting my human self react like this?

This was a first for him, reacting physically to a human woman, and he sure as hell wasn't happy about it. This primal reaction was all-male, and he didn't like the implications; it was more than a little disconcerting.

Logan knew he was in serious trouble when he felt his muscles tighten in warning; his body was preparing to shift back to man. It took a great deal of willpower and strength, but he managed to force the change to stop. He tried, unsuccessfully, to concentrate on everything that was solely Cat in him.

Hoping for an immediate distraction, Logan turned his gaze away from her bare body and focused on her face. It didn't help much. The moment his gaze met her beautiful blue-purple eyes, he was lost all over again. Damn, but this debt repayment was going to be more problematic than he'd ever anticipated.

Tara smiled sweetly at him and reached out to pat his head. He purred. It didn't help his stretched-to-the-limit nerves any to realize just how hungry that sound was. He bit back a groan when she turned away from him and wrapped a long bath towel around her delectable bareness.

Before he could even catch his breath from the feeling of acute disappointment, Tara lifted him into her arms and carried him back to the bedroom. She gently deposited him in the center of the canopy bed. He wasn't sure whether to be relieved or disappointed that she was no longer holding him so close.

Tara went to a huge, walk-in closet and opened the double doors, going inside. From his viewpoint on the bed, Logan could only hear her movements, so he let his imagination fill in the picture of her dropping that towel and getting dressed. Realizing just how dangerous his thoughts were getting, he allowed himself another pitiful meow.

The sooner this mission was over, the better. For them both.

Chapter Three

Tara finished drying her body with the towel. She grabbed her underwear from a dresser against the closet wall and slipped the silky panties and bra on. She pulled on a pair of jeans and a soft sweatshirt. Her shoulder-length hair was already starting to dry so she fluffed it with her hands and left the closet.

Going over to her vanity she picked up her comb and worked the tangles out. She knew she was stalling, doing little, unimportant things, but she couldn't get up the nerve to leave the security of her bedroom just yet. She seldom wore makeup so couldn't use that as an excuse to dally any longer in front of her mirror.

She'd put off this task for far too long. It was time to confront the situation and deal with the consequences. Dread settled in the pit of her stomach. Her family was going to be so disappointed in her, and it hurt to her soul to know she had willingly caused them to feel that way. She took a deep breath and then exhaled slowly. She turned back to face the cat.

"Well, kit. It's time. I have to face this and stop being such a coward. I think it's best if you stay here. Mother isn't going to take any of this well, and you'd be just another added problem."

The cat meowed, in his now-habitual pitiful tone, and Tara laughed. "You'll be fine." It felt good to be able to laugh, if only for a too-short moment. She doubted she'd ever have much to laugh about again …

She lifted her head, squared her shoulders, and left the bedroom. She walked down the stairs slowly and mentally counted every step as though that would somehow delay her descent.

Her parents, along with Mara and Jason, were waiting in the family room. Tara stopped just inside the arched doorway and looked from face to face. Colleen's beautiful features were drawn and tense. Lach's stern, yet handsome face showed he was more than ready to be the disciplining father. Mara and Jason simply looked disappointed.

I wish this didn't hurt so much. I never meant for them to be so disappointed in me. But, it couldn't be undone now. She'd set the course and did what she thought best for her future. It wasn't fair that Fate demanded such a high price from her. Then. And now.

"Tara, we're sorry about Mark," her father spoke first, breaking the tense silence. "Even though we did not agree to you marrying him, we never wished him harm."

Mark. Sweet, gentle, innocent man. It's still hard to believe he's gone. He'd been dying of cancer when she'd met him, but she'd always thought they would have more time together. The friendship that blossomed between them was firm and immediate, and it wasn't too long after they met that Tara realized their relationship could be taken to a more personal level … and benefit them both in their time of need. Mark had needed someone to be with him in his last days. She had needed the relationship to get her out of being the pawn for the Prophecy.

From the time she was old enough to understand, Tara had known about her destined fate and her link to the Prophecy of the Shifter Goddess. She was the Chosen One. Yet, with everything in her she had rebelled against that destiny. She had never been willing to sacrifice herself for an ageless prophecy that would demand that she give herself to a stranger—a shapeshifter—and spend her life ruling by his side as Queen.

She'd wanted a normal life. But it hadn't turned out that way. She'd been trained in the ways of the Goddess, taught all there was to know about shapeshifters, and had learned to hone the skills of magical talent that came natural to her. Every moment of her life had been planned. Without her consent.

When she'd become old enough to realize she had a will of her own, Tara had rebelled, unwilling to sacrifice her future.

Later, Mark had been an answer to her prayers, even though she had known all along it would be only temporary. That is … until this morning's revelation.

"He passed in his sleep," she told them. She walked into the room and sat down in a chair opposite her parents. "There was no pain.

And it was a blessing he had already accepted his fate." Fresh tears stung her eyes. Mark had been such a gentle man, and so accepting of death. She wished they'd had more time together.

Lach cleared his throat and shifted in his seat. "We have to ask this, Tara." He snared her tearful gaze with his hard one. Tara recognized that "don't-you-dare-lie-to-me" look. His tone was hard, stern, as he asked, "Were you and Mark ... intimate?"

Here it was. The ultimate betrayal. She choked back more tears. "Yes." She knew it was the last thing they wanted to hear. It was the last thing she wanted to have to tell them. But there was still more.

Colleen shrieked out a wail of dismay. Mara gasped, her face going pale. Jason groaned and muttered something under his breath. Her father just stared at her, his features filled with a rage that caused her heart to race.

"You defied the Fates and deliberately gave yourself to a human." He choked out the words in a tone so harsh that Tara cringed and bit back a cry of dismay. "Words can not even begin to express my disappointment and anger, young lady. You defied your parents when we forbid you to leave with him and marry him. Now, you have admitted to doing the most rebellious action of all." His voice cracked with his fury, wrought emotions emphasizing every word, "Why? Why did you do this, Tara?"

What could she say that she hadn't already said countless times before? *I wanted to choose my own future. My own ... mate. I didn't want to be a puppet for some old prophecy.* But the words remained unspoken. They were as worthless now as they had been all her life. Tara fought to hold back her tears. She blinked rapidly several times, her vision blurring. Crying wouldn't change anything, and she hated showing the weakness now. There was something else she had to tell them. And when they heard, they were going to hate her. Her stomach churned, her heartbeat increased, and her hands started sweating.

It was now or never. She forced her tone to be as firm as she could make it, despite the heartache choking her. "I found out this morning that ... I'm pregnant."

Colleen surged to her feet, uttered a hoarse cry, and then fell forward in a faint. Cursing, Lach managed to catch his wife before she hit the floor. He cuddled her close and then turned on Tara with all the rage he possessed.

"Dammit, Tara! This is too much."

Her father's cold, harsh voice sent icy chills straight through her. She'd never heard him this enraged before. She couldn't blame him, but she had harbored a small hope her parents would understand once they realized there was no turning back. Enveloping chills wracked her body as she stood up.

Lach growled out, "Go to your room. Now. I can't even bear to look at you. We will discuss this later."

She didn't hesitate. Blinded by her tears, Tara ran from the room. She fled up the stairs to the safety of her own bedroom, slammed the door close, and flung herself across her bed. Flooding tears fell, hard and fast. She buried her face against her pillow and sobbed her heart out.

Chapter Four

Logan listened to her heart-wrenching crying until he couldn't stand it any more. He didn't know what was wrong, but her sobs were tearing his heart to pieces. He could feel her pain as if it was his own. Every male instinct in him was hammering for him to change back to a man and take her in his arms, comfort her, protect her. It definitely wasn't the smartest thing he could do at the moment, so he forced back the need and moved up the bed to sit down by her shaking shoulders. He nuzzled her shoulder and purred softly, scooting in as close as he could get to her. Blinded by tears, Tara reached out and pulled him closer, cuddling her face against him. She cried harder.

Damn. If she doesn't stop crying, I'm going to change back and go kill someone for causing this. He knew the thought was irrational but he didn't care. He couldn't stand the way her crying was affecting him. Possessive, protective emotions surged through him, unexpected and unwanted. He couldn't remember a time in his entire life when he'd felt this way about anyone, especially a human woman.

He had to stop thinking like this. It was dangerous territory he had no business stepping into. Still, the need to change battered at his senses. To keep from allowing the change to come over him, Logan settled against Tara and purred louder, harder. He nuzzled his head under her chin, rubbing at the delicate spot of her throat, and purred nonstop.

A long while later, Tara's tears lessened. His purrs were louder than her soft hiccups now. But he continued with the comforting sound and they lay like that for over an hour. Tara cuddled him close, and he purred so long that his throat got sore. He didn't care; he'd do anything to stop her tears.

After a long while, Tara brushed the tears off her cheeks and sat up. Logan curled onto her lap with one last comforting purr. She sniffled a few times, shivered once or twice, and softly petted his head. Her touch was oddly sensual to his over-heated senses and Logan had to keep reminding himself that he was in cat form and she wasn't purposely trying to drive him crazy.

Tara sighed, the sound wrenching. Logan wanted to growl. "Oh, kit. I think I've ruined my life. How could I have hurt them so much? I was selfish, and didn't care that this would change their lives as much as it would mine."

Logan waited, hoping for an explanation. Whatever the problem was, he knew she would have to settle it before he could risk exposing himself. He wanted her cooperation, not a fight, and right now she wasn't in the best of receptive moods for such a startling revelation. Patience was always hard-won for Logan, and right now he was feeling the strain of having to wait. A deep gut instinct told him that the longer he was with Tara, the more complicated things were going to become.

Tara didn't help any by not offering further information. Instead, she lay back down and cuddled him close against her once again. She sighed, the sound tearful and gut-wrenching to him, and Logan started purring again. At this rate, his throat would be raw before morning.

A torturous half hour later, Tara fell asleep. He listened to her soft breathing for a long time. He lifted his head and his gaze caressed over her beautiful features. She looked like a sweet angel, alluring yet oh-so-innocent. Her soft, curly, sun-blonde hair fell in disarray around her angelic face, some of the silky locks resting against his head. He wanted to brush the hair back from her face, caress over the appealing softness of her skin, touch her cheeks, and feather his fingers over her sensuous pink lips. The urge was so strong, so hot, that the need to change flowed through him like an erupting volcano.

He didn't have a choice. He had to change now. Logan jumped from the bed and trotted to the door. He had one fleeting moment to hope that Tara was a deep sleeper before his body started morphing from cat to man. The change was instantaneous, and he mentally willed on a pair of jeans, T-shirt, and boots. He grunted at the irony: he was damned lucky that shifters had the power to do that, or he would have been in a real predicament right now. He hadn't planned on being trapped here with Tara that long, and certainly not trapped in her bedroom in his cat form.

Luck was on his side again when he cautiously opened the bedroom door and found the hall in darkness. It was late, and hopefully the family was already in their beds. He glanced once more at Tara, who slept blissfully unaware of him, and stepped out of the room. He closed the door behind him and then glanced both ways down the hall. His preternatural senses assured him that no one was stirring in the big house, and he breathed a sigh of relief.

Downstairs, he found his way to the front door and was thankful to discover that although there was a security box on the wall next to the door, the alarm had not been set.

He briefly thought about the false security humans allowed themselves; a shifter home was always heavily guarded and safely secured.

Outside, Logan breathed in the night air. Varied, country scents teased his senses. It called to his animal side, tempting him with the need to run ... and hunt. He realized he was hungry, but decided that would have to wait. Like a stealthy shadow passing quickly through the night's darkness, he jogged across the wide lawn and straight into the nearby orchard. He'd left a backpack there earlier when he'd scouted out Tara's home before going out to meet her.

He found the bag where he'd left it beneath an overgrown cherry tree. He pulled out his cell phone, flipped it open and punched the speed dial number programmed in.

A male voice instantly answered. "Austin here."

"Do you have any updates?" Logan asked without preamble.

"Sorry, Logan. Nothing. We did a complete research file on Mark Coons and there wasn't anything more than we already knew. He was thirty-five, had bone cancer, and was fully human. Tara met him in Salt Lake City at an art gallery. They married two weeks after meeting. Three months later, he died." Austin shuffled papers as he read on. "We verified that he was an only child, parents dead, and no other living, close relatives. This guarantees us that there's no one on his side of the family who will search for Tara."

Logan's gut instinct was telling him that something just wasn't right. He'd been so careful in planning this mission, but everything was going smoother than he'd anticipated. So far, the only major obstacle he'd run into was Tara. It was bad enough she'd married a human. What would this mean now for Damian and the Prophecy? Did she still retain her Goddess-to-be powers or had marrying and becoming intimate with a human annulled those powers? He grimaced, not liking that train of thought.

He couldn't let himself dwell on it. He was honor-bound to deliver her to Damian and that was what he would do. If things kept going this well, he'd get her to Damian in two night's time at the latest.

"Keep me posted. If you discover anything else, call me on this cell number," he told Austin, then closed the phone. He wasn't expecting any more set backs, but Logan was prepared. He would have to expose himself to Tara soon, possibly tomorrow, and then convince her to leave with him. He had a bad feeling that was going to be a lot harder than he thought.

Her family obviously hadn't reacted well to her marriage. Hell, he didn't blame them. She had just turned twenty, and from what he'd discovered about her, she was as innocent as a new-born babe. She'd been protected and secluded from the world all her life. Her rebellious act of getting married was a blow to the family. And if they were aware of the Prophecy, then it was even more of a disaster for all involved. That explained Tara's tears. Apparently her family's disappointment had been very demonstrative.

Logan rubbed at the ache in his throat. He grinned. He'd never purred that long or that hard anytime in his life. A little soreness was worth it; he'd do it again if she ever needed him to.

He glanced up at the moon, estimating the time of night. His stomach rumbled, reminding him that he hadn't eaten since early that morning. He had enough time to change back to lion form and hunt, and then be back on Tara's bed before she or the rest of the family woke in the morning.

Hunting in lion form was just what he needed. It would keep his mind from thoughts he was better off not thinking about. With just a willed thought, his body began the transformation. Clothes disappeared in the blink of an eye. Limbs, muscles, and skin, all morphed into the mountain lion in just mere moments.

He shook his large head, and lifted his nose to scent the air for prey. He could smell rabbits, deer, and other country animals, and his cat instincts sprang to life. He lifted his head and roared into the darkness of the night—the lion was on the hunt.

He glided like a stealthy, ominous shadow through the orchard grove, and then further on into the surrounding woods. His last human thought was that for this short time he was free. Free of human thoughts and emotions. Free to be the beast he was born to be.

•

Tara woke with a headache and a queasy stomach. And to the comforting sound of soft purring in her ear. She smiled and reached out to touch the big yellow cat reclining on her pillow next to her head. She scratched lightly behind his ear. "Good morning, kit."

The cat meowed in answer and then leaned in to touch his nose to hers. She giggled. "What a sweet thing you are."

She sat up slowly, careful not to upset her stomach any more than it already was. She rubbed at the ache in her temples. "I almost wish it wasn't morning already," she told the cat. "I was having the strangest dream, yet it was the most comforting one I've ever had. You were in it, kit. I was walking around this dark place, lost, scared, and crying. Then you showed up." She glanced down at the cat and grinned. "But then you changed into a lion. Lucky for me, you were a nice one. I instinctively knew I shouldn't be afraid of you. Then, you carried me on your back out of the darkness."

She got out of bed and headed to the bathroom. "I can't believe I would have such a wistful, comforting dream after the last few days I've been through."

She grimaced. If she thought the last few days had been rough, she couldn't imagine getting through the next ones. Last night's confrontation with her family had shown her that she was on her own in this situation. She just wished she knew what to do to make things easier for them all. She couldn't change the past, but she could work for their forgiveness. If … they were only willing to give her that chance.

She'd been raised to respect and to accept the Goddess's decree. Unlike Mara, whose devotion to the Goddess was unwavering and strongly instilled in her, she was the rebellious one who wanted more than just a destiny already chosen for her before her birth.

Tara showered and dressed, then came out of the bathroom to comb the tangles out of her freshly shampooed hair. She took her time, knowing she was stalling. She had to face them sooner or later, and it would be better to do it now instead of dreading the inevitable for any longer. She leaned down and kissed the cat on the top of his head. "I'll bring you some food later, kit. Be good and stay here."

He gave her his normal pitiful meow and she laughed then kissed his head again. He purred his appreciation in a loud tone. When she left the room she realized that she was still smiling. Kit had come into her life just at the right time—when she needed his comforting presence the most.

She found the family in the breakfast room. Their silence was ominous and cold, slicing immediately through to her very soul. A heavy weight of despair settled over her once again. She entered and sat down at her usual place at the table. She looked from beloved face to face but no one looked back at her. She wanted to cry.

Her stomach quivered, protesting at the smell of the food on the table. She pushed down the rising flare of panic. Vomiting now would only bring unwanted attention to the problem she was facing. She reached for her glass and forced a few swallows of water down her throat. Her stomach instantly rebelled. It took her several deep breaths and calming exhales before she was able to clear her throat of the bile.

She looked at her family again. She had to be the one to break the silence. "I'm sorry."

For long moments, no one answered her. Hot tears burned in her eyes but she resolutely blinked them away. *I will not cry again. Not now.* It certainly wouldn't change anything; her tears had been ignored last night. She'd just have to find a way to deal with this, no matter what the cost, no matter how much their rejection hurt. And it hurt. More than she'd ever thought possible.

Colleen raised her head and looked at her. Her motherly voice was calm and Tara was unable to discern her mood. "Tara, you must try to eat something." She placed a slice of toast on a small plate and handed it across the table to her.

Tara took the plate but set it down next to her water glass. She couldn't stomach the thought of food right then. And the chilling atmosphere in the room was getting more bitter cold by the moment. It was seeping through to her bones, chilling her to her soul. It hurt more than anything else had ever done in her life. She didn't think she could take it much longer. She had to say something, now, before the silence and cold killed her.

"I have to know." She raised her chin, met their stares with as much courage as she could muster. "Are you ever going to be able to forgive me? It's done now and there's no turning back. I ... need my family." She ran a shaky hand over her eyes to brush away the stubborn tears that threatened to fall. "Don't you understand? This is my life and I had to make the decision to do what I thought was best."

"Best?" Lach bit the word out like a growl. "You can't even comprehend what's best for you, Tara. Your destiny was ordained, planned before your birth by a Goddess who loved you enough to choose you as one of her special children. Your willful rebellion is a direct insult to the Goddess and to your family." He slammed his fist down on the table, making the plates and glasses rattle. "I cannot believe a child of mine would be so disrespectful."

"I didn't want to marry a beast!"

There. She'd said it. Screamed it, actually. And it got their attention. Colleen and Mara both gasped in dismay. Jason frowned so hard he looked like dynamite ready to explode. Lach turned pale despite the rage heating his blood to a boiling point.

She spoke softly this time, trying hard to make them understand, "I couldn't stand the thought of spending my life married to a man who is half beast and who would expect me to live in his world. How could you want that of me?"

"This is my fault," Colleen whispered, her voice tearful. "I should have talked to you about this when you first learned of your destiny. I could have prepared you better."

"Prepared me?" Tara shook her head. "How do you prepare to give up a life of normalcy in exchange for a life of ... supernatural living? And it's not just the lifestyle either, Mother. You know that I'm talking about. Being ... intimate with the shifter who would be my husband." She turned to her father, her words hard and accusing, "And you would willingly sacrifice your daughter to that situation for a prophecy?"

Lach stared at her and Tara tried hard to see into his soul, to know what he was feeling at that moment. His next words told her everything.

"Yes."

Her heart sank. Her soul cried. He had always been a hard father, but he had loved her. Or so she thought. Had her whole life been worth nothing to him except the means to fulfill a prophecy for the Goddess he worshipped?

Tara felt defeated. Completely exhausted. It was as if every ounce of fight she'd had in her was gone and nothing mattered anymore.

She had to get away from here. She stood up and pushed her chair back from the table. She met their stares with her head held high.

"I'm sorry I failed you. But I wouldn't change anything I've done. You don't have to understand, or forgive me, but I hope that your disappointment never turns to … hate. I couldn't bear that."

She looked at her sister. Mara's blue eyes were teary, and compassion covered her lovely features. Deep in her heart she knew that her sister loved her and was trying hard to understand her decisions. Mara's devotion to the Goddess had never faltered, and she had never rebelled against her destiny. As of yet, the Goddess had not announced what Mara's fate would be, and Tara felt heartsick with the possibility that her sister might now be chosen to take her place in this marriage arrangement.

"I hope my decision doesn't hurt you, Mara," she told her. "I couldn't bear that, either."

"I'll be fine, Tara. We'll get through this," Mara answered gently, "I know we will."

Tara gave her a heartfelt smile of gratitude and love. "I know we can't change this, but I'm willing to try and make amends. Somehow."

"Tell that to the Goddess," Lach stated.

Tara cringed at his harsh tone. She knew her father was never going to forgive her, and the pain of that knowledge would never leave her. Her heart was breaking, she could feel it sharply crumbling into little pieces.

There wasn't anything else she could say or do. She would live with her decision. But not here. This wasn't home anymore and she knew it.

She lifted her head, squared her shoulders, and walked out of the room.

Twenty minutes later she placed a suitcase and the cat in her car and drove away. She refused to look back.

Chapter Five

Logan wasn't laying bets they would get to any destination safe and in one piece. Tara cried in wrenching sobs as she drove, and the sounds were heartbreaking as tears flowed down her face and soaked her blouse. He mentally crossed his paw fingers hoping she could see clearly enough to keep the car on the road.

Her crying was killing him. In just the short time he'd been around her he had discovered that her tears could do things to him he didn't like—make him feel emotions he was better off not having in the first place. He wanted to change back to a man and hold her in his arms, comfort her, protect her from all the hurt the world was throwing her way right now.

I should go back there and beat the hell out of her father. What kind of man puts his religious beliefs ahead of the welfare of one of his children?

Logan had never thought about having children. Shapeshifters married shifters, for obvious reasons, and he had yet to meet a female that inspired that kind of commitment from him. He'd had lovers, but had always made sure he'd never allowed the mating process to occur during sex. When he did one day find that special mate, she would have to be someone very unique. She would be strong, intelligent, a shifter worthy to reign by his side as leader of the Cat Clans. He wouldn't settle for anything less. Once he found her, he would do anything and everything in his power to claim her. But until then, he was willing to play the field and stay away from any serious relationships.

That's why his attraction, his possessiveness of Tara was so disconcerting. He didn't know how to deal with it—didn't even want to think about it.

He watched Tara as she made a valiant effort to control her tears. She was so humanly fragile, but she had the strength of courage that went deep. It was one of the traits he admired most in a woman. She would make a worthy mate. Damian Sinclair was one lucky shifter.

Damnation. Don't even go there! He had no right to be thinking what he was thinking. She belonged to Damian. He had to keep remembering that. And, too, she was human. A human woman had no place in his world.

Not for the first time, he wondered why the Shifter Goddess had chosen a human for Damian. Logan frowned. He wished they knew more about the Prophecy. What if there was something vital they were missing by not knowing exactly what the decree was for all the shifter clans? What if there was a specific reason humans were involved now?

Tara suddenly braked, and then swerved the car to the side of the road. Taken by surprise, Logan spit out an angry yowl of protest as the car's momentum threw him off the seat and onto the floor. He straightened his tangled limbs and then swung around to glare up at Tara. She fumbled with the car door for a moment before falling halfway out. She managed to get to her feet and then she stumbled away from the car. Logan saw her disappear into the wooded area off the side of the road.

He jumped up on the seat and then out of the open car door. He followed her retreating scent, and found her yards away. He saw her fall to her knees as she gasped in dry heaves and bent over clutching her stomach.

That was the final straw. Her pain was breaking his heart. He changed back to a man instantly, and had one last coherent thought to will on clothes. He knew he would scare her, suddenly appearing like this, but he wasn't about to let her suffer through this alone. Every primal, male instinct in him was screaming with the need to take her in his arms and protect her from this pain.

Logan approached her on silent tread. He stopped a few feet behind her. He clenched his hands into fists and forced himself not to go to her. Softly, he called out her name.

She reacted with a startled gasp and swung her head around to face him. Logan quickly held his arms out from in his body in a non-threatening stance. He made his voice as soft and as gentle as possible, "I'm not going to hurt you, sweetheart. I just want to help."

Maybe this hadn't been a good idea after all. Tara's beautiful eyes widened in shocked fear. Before he could take the few steps to reach her, she fell forward into a faint.

Logan cursed at his stupidity and strode to her. He gently lifted her in his arms. She was so light, and much too fragile. Her head lolled back against his shoulder and he noted the unnatural paleness of her skin. He tightened his protective hold. "I'm sorry, angel. I should have done this some other way." Mentally cursing himself for every kind of fool, he carried his precious burden back to the car.

He sat her in the passenger-side seat and buckled the seatbelt around her limp form. He moved her head to a more comfortable position, and then gently pushed back wayward curls from her face to tuck them behind her ears. His fingers lingered on the incredible softness of her skin, caressed over her cheeks, and then feathered down to her lips. Something ... hot and wild stirred to life deep inside him. Replacing the protectiveness was an uncontrollable possessiveness that had his head reeling with the force of it.

With a surge of desperate willpower, Logan pulled his hands away from her and clenched them into fists. He straightened, closed the car door, and walked to the driver's side. He started the car without even glancing at Tara again. He knew they were less than an hour from Salt Lake City. He'd take her there and get a motel room for the night. She needed to recover and ... he needed time to get better control of his wayward thoughts.

He clenched the steering wheel with a grip that had his knuckles turning white.

He was in a killing mood.

•

An hour later, his mood had changed to deep worry. Despite the time that had passed, Tara still hadn't regained consciousness. She remained unconscious when he carried her into the room he'd rented at the out-of-the-way motel off the freeway. He'd chosen the motel because of its unremarkable appearance and location. He wanted to avoid all possible attention. He just hoped that no one saw him carrying a woman into the room. Might as well be shouting, "Look!" Luck was on his side with the fact the parking lot had only two other cars and they were parked on the far end of the building from this room.

His gaze kept a watchful perusing of the area as he pushed the motel room door open with his booted foot. His senses couldn't detect anything out of the ordinary, anywhere near, and he breathed a sigh of relief. For now, there wasn't another shifter in the area—yet. He grimaced.

He kicked the door closed behind him and carried Tara to the only bed in the room. Gently depositing her there, he stepped back away from her and stared down at her pale, reposed features. He had the urge to caress her face again but fought against it; the need to touch her was becoming a relentless, drugging habit he hadn't been aware of until now. But nonetheless, he recognized it for the need it was, and knew he had to fight it with every ounce of willpower he possessed.

He stared down at her. It wasn't hard to see she carried Goddess genes. Her beauty was ethereal. It was the first thing he'd noticed about her. Logan grinned. The second thing he'd noticed was that she was incredibly sexy, with all those tempting curves on a body any man couldn't help but desire.

He ran a shaky hand over his face. Damn, but he had to stop thinking these thoughts. He had to keep reminding himself that not only was she a human but she also belonged to Damian. His mind agreed with the logic, but his body protested with the urge to touch her again.

He leaned down and gently caressed her soft cheek. His voice was gruff as he whispered, "Poor angel, you're exhausted. Mentally as well as physically. I should be shot for my reactions to you. You don't need me adding to the complications of your life right now."

He straightened away from her. Letting her sleep was the best thing for her. And it kept him more on guard. He groaned. He had to be one sick puppy—er, cat—to be lusting after a woman as vulnerable as Tara was right now.

He left the room and went back to the car to retrieve her suitcase, and his backpack that he'd stashed in the backseat the night before. He perused the area again. An uneasy feeling of being watched made the hairs on the back of his neck stand in warning. He lifted his head and sniffed the air. Nothing unusual floated on the invisible waves so he had to believe it was just him being edgy.

Goddess knew he had enough reasons to be edgy right now. The sooner he delivered Tara to Damian the better he'd feel. Just when things had become so complicated, he wasn't sure, but he knew he was going to have to fight his growing attraction to Tara before it became something more.

He blamed his lack of awareness and habitual on-guard stance, for what happened next. If he'd only been his usual alert self, he would have never ended up on the floor of the room with a loud ringing in his ears from the sudden blow to his head.

Chapter Six

Tara slowly opened her eyes and groaned as a bright light greeted her blurred vision. She lay still for a long moment trying to recall what had happened. Panic threatened, and she forced the emotion back down. She closed her eyes and tried to concentrate on the last coherent moment she could remember.

… the heart wrenching departure from her family and home … crying so hard as she drove away that she thought her heart would break in two … the overwhelming nausea that had forced her to stop the car and run into the bushes … hearing someone call her name … turning around … seeing the stranger approach her …

She surged up in bed so fast her vision swam. When it cleared she could see that she was in a small nondescript room. One fearful glance around, and at the open-door bathroom, confirmed she was alone. For the moment.

But, where was here? She chewed on her bottom lip, her gaze flying to the door. The more important question was where was the stranger?

A trembling started down deep in her body. Every nerve in her body was tingling in warning that she was in danger. She left the bed and walked over to the curtained window. She risked a careful peek out. Her car was the only one parked near the row of rooms of the dowdy motel with the sign *Snow Mountain Inn*.

Her gaze flew back to her car. The stranger! He was coming towards the room with long purposeful strides, a determined look on his handsome features.

He was tall, well over six feet. His body was athletic-slim; his dark blue t-shirt hugged his wide chest, and the black jeans fit smugly over his long legs and narrow hips. His long hair was brandy-brown, thick, and curled slightly at the ends over his shoulders. His face was a tanned work of art, chiseled in stark handsomeness.

And he was almost at the door now! Panic overwhelmed her. She swung away from the window and searched the small room for some kind of weapon. *I'll strike first, and ask questions later.*

It never occurred to her to simply lock the door. Her thoughts were so panic-filled that she wasn't even aware of running around the room in circles frantically looking for some object to use as defense until she heard his booted footsteps right outside the door. She grabbed the only thing within her reach: a small table lamp.

She rushed to stand in a defensive stance next to the door and held the lamp as high as she could. Her nerves sang with fear, her breathing was catchy, and her hands shook. Every bit of self defense she had been taught flew right out of her mind.

The door opened and Tara's heart raced. With a grunt of determination she struck, aiming for his head.

He was too tall, and her strike missed its intended mark. She slammed the lamp into the side of his head and he went down.

But only for a moment.

With a rough shake of his head the man sprang to his feet. He yanked the lamp out of her hand before she even had the chance to blink or catch her breath. She'd never seen anyone move that fast before. Despite his obvious head injury, he was very agile.

Tara realized she was staring at him in complete awe with her mouth open, jaws slack. She muttered a squeak of "Uh oh," and closed her mouth. She started to back away but realized the door was at her back and now closed.

"Why the hell did you do that?" the stranger demanded. He rubbed at the side of his head and glared daggers at her through narrowed, slightly slanted eyes of deepest blue.

Tara couldn't help but stare. Her thoughts were like scattering clouds, and she felt oddly mesmerized by his intent glare. Were men supposed to have lashes that long? She shook her head to clear the bemused thoughts. Her earlier sense of danger returned full force. She studied him closely and suddenly realized that the fear of danger wasn't coming from him. She felt it, elsewhere, and that made her even more frightened. She just wasn't as sure if he had anything to do with it too, or not.

She cleared her throat and forced her voice to be as strong as she could make it. She had the feeling that showing any kind of fear wasn't the best idea.

"What did you expect me to do?" she demanded, placing her hands on her hips and glaring back. "Just be sitting here, meekly waiting for you to return?"

He blinked in surprise at her show of bravado. Then he muttered, "Still sleeping—meekly—would have been better for us both."

Tara's overloaded senses responded to his deep, rough voice. The tone caressed over her, despite his obvious anger. She trembled with the unfamiliar touch of desire that flared over her then. She couldn't think straight, and that was a first. What was it about this man?

She shook her head. She had to get out of here. Now. Hands behind her back she slid them across the smooth wood of the door to the handle. The stranger glared at her, his sensuous mouth a thin slash of warning.

"Don't even think about it, angel. I guarantee you that I can catch you before you take a few steps out that door."

She didn't doubt him. There was something about him that made her think of a dangerous animal ready to spring at any moment on his chosen prey. And right now, she was that prey. So, where did that leave her? Who was he, and why had he kidnapped her?

He advanced toward her and she cringed not knowing what to expect. He lightly grasped her waist with both his large hands and moved her away from the door. He then slid the lock home, and slowly turned back to face her. The strange glow in his slanted eyes made her catch her breath all over again.

She was dismayed to hear her voice crack as she demanded, "Who are you, and why am I here?"

To her complete surprise, he chuckled. "There's no need for you to feel like the classical kidnapped victim, Tara. This situation is odd, I admit. But you don't have anything to fear from me."

He indicated the chair next to the bed. "Sit down, and I'll explain."

Tara sat, but only because she was feeling very uncomfortable with him towering over her so close. She'd let him explain, and then she would get away from here, no matter what she had to do.

He leaned back against the dresser by the door, and folded his arms in a casual stance across his chest. "My name is Logan Cross. I've been chosen to be your escort to your fiancé, Damian Sinclair."

Tara gasped, her heart plummeting to her feet. Although she

had never met him she knew the name of the man the Goddess had chosen as her future husband. She knew that he was the chosen Prince of the Wolf Shifter Clans and that his union with her would bring about a shift of power and control that had never been present in the Clans before now.

She couldn't believe this was happening. After all she'd done to avoid being a pawn in the Goddess's Prophecy she hadn't managed to escape her destined fate after all. *No. I won't allow this. I won't give up. I can't.*

Another thought reared to life. She protectively placed her hand over her flat stomach. *I've already given myself to another. I carry his child. The Prophecy can't be fulfilled.* This was all just a simple mistake; surely the Goddess knew of her condition and wouldn't expect her to go ahead with her union with Damian?

She lifted her head and looked deep into Logan's eyes. "I'm sorry you have made this trip for no reason. I'm already married. Damian can't claim me now."

Logan shook his head at her declaration. "I know about Mark," he stated. He moved over to sit on the edge of the bed next to the chair. He was so close. Too close. Her nerves tightened again in stark awareness of the sensual vibrations radiating off him. She didn't like this reaction to him; it wasn't natural considering the circumstances.

She had loved Mark, but hadn't been in love with him. Theirs had been more of a mutual need and friendship. She'd never experienced sexual feelings before, not even when Mark had made love to her that one and only time. Her sheltered life hadn't allowed the chance for any relationship with another man. She had to remain chaste.

Now, she was feeling things that scared her. Logan's closeness was tantalizing. She wanted to reach out and touch him, the urge so strong that she clenched her hands in her lap.

She deliberately pushed away the unwanted response to this enigmatic man. It was time to straighten this whole situation out so she could get out of here. She took a deep breath and let it out before announcing, "Do you also know that I'm pregnant with his child?"

Her words hung like invisible icicles in the room.

Logan's features darkened, anger making his eyes glint like blue sapphire. "What the hell are you talking about?"

Tara didn't know whether to be smug with her revelation or

to be frightened. Logan's anger was palpable in the space between them; she'd never experienced anything like it as it rolled in waves off him and onto her. Was she in any danger from this man? No, she reasoned. Damian wouldn't have sent him if there was a chance he would hurt her. She knew how valuable she was to the Wolf Prince and the Prophecy.

Logan surged to his feet and stalked towards her. Her heart beat sped up and her breath caught in her throat. Alarm bells went off in her mind. He towered over her and it took every ounce of willpower she had not to cower.

Logan knelt down in front of her and placed his hands on the arms of the chair, effectively caging her in. He leaned in close to her and his nostrils flared as he took in a deep ... sniff. She was taken aback by the odd action. He sniffed her? What ...? Sudden realization dawned. He must be a wolf shifter. Damian obviously wouldn't have sent a human.

A barely audible growl rumbled from his throat. He sat back on his haunches and snared her gaze with his gleaming one. "You're not pregnant."

He stated the words in a deep satisfying tone that immediately grated on her nerves like nothing else had. Jerk!

"Guess again, wolfie boy," she muttered sarcastically. Who did he think he was, a doctor? Granted, she hadn't confirmed the pregnancy with a doctor but she was experiencing all the typical symptoms: missed period, nausea, hormonal-based emotions. She had purposely had sex with Mark to insure a pregnancy. It was the only way she could think of to effectively void the Prophecy. She glared at Logan's triumphant expression. "Your senses, albeit a bit odd for using as a pregnancy test, are wrong."

Logan grinned at her, showing his teeth. She couldn't believe his audacity! She frowned at him and resisted the urge to smack that smug look off his handsome face. Barely. Her palms itched with the urge and she was lifting her hand when his gaze turned suddenly hot and ... all too thorough as it roamed over her, head to toes. The searing look stopped to focus on her stomach.

"I'm not wrong, angel," he rumbled softly. "Shifters can tell these things. We know when the time is right for a pregnancy. We know when a pregnancy is real. And we know when—"

He made a choking sound. His grin disappeared to be replaced with a hard, angry slash of his mouth. His eyes glinted with a dangerous light. He leaned in and took another sniff of her, this time longer, closer, almost touching her nose with his.

Logan drew back and spit out a foul curse. He surged to his feet and backed away from her. His entire body went stiff.

"Damn! Hell! Not that! Not now. Lousy timing!" He spun away from her and started pacing in long, angry strides across the room. He muttered foul words in between a colorful rant that had her blushing. She'd never heard such words in all her life!

"So much for a life-debt," he ground out, pacing like a caged animal. "I'm going to kill him. I'm going to kill the shifter who saved my life. He'll never see it coming. I'll rip his damn throat out and feed it to the rest of his pack."

Tara stared at him, total fascination swamping her senses. She was all too aware of his primal strength and power; it flowed off him in searing hot waves. His muscles rippled under the tight T-shirt as he stomped in long strides back and forth waving his hands. He was every bit a wild animal right then, dangerous, unpredictable. She couldn't tear her gaze from him.

Some little voice deep in her conscience had to ask if Damian was as wild and powerful as Logan. Would he set her heart racing hard like Logan was doing now? Would her husband-to-be make her tremble with this unaccustomed desire, too?

Husband-to-be. The words echoed in her mind like an aggravating chant of doom. This was really happening. Everything she and Mark had done was for naught. She was being taken to Damian.

Wait a minute. What had Logan just said? Why was he acting so enraged? She glared at his pacing figure. "What did you mean by 'not that?'"

His stride or ranting never faltered. So she tried again, this time making her voice a little louder and firmer. "If you don't stop with all the foul words, I'm going to find a bar of soap and wash your mouth out."

There! That worked. He abruptly stopped in the middle of the room and swung around to glare ferociously at her. She met his angry stare with more bravado than she actually felt. He looked like she was something foul tasting in his mouth. *This can't be good.*

•

Logan swallowed down a string of expletives that would have

made even the toughest man blush. He couldn't believe this was happening. Of all the complications or problems he'd anticipated in this situation, what he'd just discovered wasn't one of them.

Had Damian known? Is that why he'd chosen this particular time to claim Tara? He'd made the point of warning Logan about the danger of other wolf shifters trying to claim her, but he'd never come right out and said why!

Logan took in a deep breath and released it on a long exhale. His nostrils flared as her sweet, womanly scent teased his senses. Why hadn't he noticed it before now? Maybe he had noticed, but had just rationalized that it was a basic animal attraction to the opposite sex. No, that wasn't the reason; his attraction to her had started when he'd first met her. This particular situation had to have only started within the last hour.

He ran a hand over his face, feeling more tense than he'd ever felt in his entire life. The room was too small, too closed in. And she smelled … too damn good! He swallowed a lustful groan. How the hell was he supposed to handle this?

He was going to kill Damian for putting him in this situation. Fool! Didn't he realize that even though Logan was a cat shifter, he'd still be just as susceptible? Hell, any man, shifter or otherwise, would be!

Logan squared his shoulders. He had to get control. Now. Or there was sure to be hell to pay. His thoughts flew in different directions as he tried to logically come up with a solution.

But his too-acute senses were on full alert. And every breath he took made him more aware of the woman he was honor bound to deliver to another man.

A woman, whose essence was already so deeply imbedded in him, body and soul. And would be, forever.

Chapter Seven

Tara watched the myriad of odd emotions pass over Logan's features. She alternated between being frightened and fascinated. She was exhausted too, and more so now than she could ever remember being. She needed to get a handle on all this and figure out what to do next.

"Why are you acting as though I've suddenly turned into a leper or something else?" Logan was still keeping his distance after that last outburst, and she was beginning to get a little scared.

His voice was low and strained, "We've got a problem, angel." He ran his hand over his face again, and then exhaled loudly. "And I'm not sure how to deal with it."

Tara didn't like the sound of that. "I'm already confused," she muttered. "Can you please explain more?"

Logan grunted. "Damn. I might as well come out and say it." His voice changed to something rougher, deeper. "You're in heat, Tara. Ripe. Ready to be mated."

Tara gasped. She felt her cheeks heat with instant embarrassment. In heat! It was the last thing she'd expected him to say. She choked out a little laugh. "Well, that was a bit crude."

"Sorry."

"Right. Not only did that sound insincere, but you're looking at me like it's my fault and I'm doing this deliberately." And did he have to look so pained about it? She didn't know whether to be embarrassed or angry.

She thought back over the past week. The false symptoms of pregnancy were obviously her body preparing for her cycle. Her mother had told her that when the time came, her body would prepare itself for the special mating between her and the wolf shifter.

Logan's intense stare made her embarrassment deepen. This should be a discussion between her and Damian. Not a perfect stranger! "It's really none of your business what's going on with my body right now," she stated, meeting his stare. "You're just the delivery boy. You don't need to concern yourself about anything else."

Uh oh. Maybe she shouldn't have called him that.

Delivery guy or not, this obviously wasn't a man who tolerated much from anyone. He looked ready to hit something. Or someone! Oddly enough, she wasn't afraid. A deep-soul instinct told her that Logan would never willingly hurt her. She didn't know why she was so sure of this, but the feeling was more real than any she had ever had.

"Let's get things straight here, Tara." Logan's deep tone was filled with hard derisiveness. "I'm no one's delivery boy. Damian asked me to escort you for a specific reason." His hot stare caressed over her from head to toes. "I can understand now that it was for several reasons. The main reason is your—state of health. He must have thought you'd be safer with me than with one of his own kind."

"One of his own kind?" What was that suppose to mean? Was Logan saying he wasn't a wolf shifter, that he was fully human? She couldn't believe a human would be involved in this; so few knew of the existence of the supernatural.

Logan exhaled a rough sigh. "I'm not a wolf shifter. I'm Head of the Cat Clan in Washington."

"A cat?" Tara knew she was repeating his words again, but she couldn't think straight. "I didn't realize that the Cat and Wolf Clans got along so well with each other. Why did Damian choose you?"

"Long story," he muttered. She got the distinct impression that he didn't want to elaborate so she clamped her mouth shut before asking any more questions. She didn't want to antagonize him any more than necessary.

Her first priority was to figure out what she was going to do. Did Logan believe that she would willingly go with him? Damian's arrogance had obviously made him think that she could be summoned when the time came. Well, both men were wrong! She wasn't going to go like a willing lamb to the slaughter.

She had to get away from Logan. She glanced around the small room and saw her suitcase lying on the table beside the bed. Her cell phone was in her purse that must be still in the car. Most likely her car keys were in his pocket. Running didn't seem like a good option when she considered that she probably wouldn't get far without phone or keys. She frowned. Who would she go to for help, anyway? Her family would gratefully hand her right back to Logan, or personally escort her to Damian. If she called the police for help, they'd think she was crazy. Telling them her story was definitely out of the question.

Staring at her suitcase made her feel something was missing besides just her purse. She glanced around the room again, and then asked, "You didn't leave Kit in the car, did you?"

"Kit?" Logan looked confused for a moment. And then comprehension dawned and he smiled. "Oh. *That* kit. Actually, he's right here."

It only took her a moment to figure out what he was saying. The cat had been him all along! Indignant anger surged deep inside her. He was a cat shifter. What better way than to get in her good graces than showing up as an injured cat needing her help.

"You were with me all that time and never had the decency to reveal yourself? What were you doing? Spying?" Her thoughts flew back over the last twenty-four hours. Oh no. She had been naked in front of him! "I think I'm going to kill you," she stated, dead calm despite the embarrassment and anger flooding her. He didn't even have the decency to look repentant! Her palm itched with the urge to smack him. She'd never wanted to hit someone so much in her life.

"Sorry about that," he said, not sounding sorry at all. His grin was wolfish, and his eyes shone like dark sapphires. "I had my reasons for not revealing my identity too soon." His hot gaze caressed over her, making her feel like he'd physically touched her. "I didn't expect you to be naked anytime."

"You bastard!"

He shook his head and wagged a finger at her. "Now, angel. That's not the type of words that should be coming out of a Goddess's mouth."

"You'd better be very thankful that I don't have my Goddess powers yet," she threatened. "Or you would be in serious, bad shape right now."

"I'm shaking in my boots."

Tara clenched her hands into tight fists. Vivid, mental pictures of what she'd do to him for revenge flashed through her mind. She'd turn him into a permanent cat and see how he liked that!

She grimaced. Too bad she really didn't have those types of powers. Instead she used the only weapon she could think of; her voice dripped with the obvious threat, "I don't think that Damian is going to be happy to know you saw me like that."

•

Logan growled low in his throat. She was right, dammit. He knew if he was in Damian's place, he'd kill any man or shifter who dared take advantage of his mate and do what he had. The thought of anyone, including Damian, seeing Tara in all her naked glory was enough to shoot a fountain of rage through his entire body.

Hell. When had he become so damned possessive of her? She belonged to someone else. He had to keep reminding himself of that.

He wanted to blame his volatile emotions on the sweet, enticing pheromones emitting from Tara. A woman in heat was enough to drive any shifter crazy. The animal side of their nature was more sensitive to the situation. But he knew, deep down inside him, it wasn't just her condition that had him wanting her with a need so acute his body felt on fire. It was Tara herself.

Logan wanted to hit something. Or someone. Damian's face came into his mind. He couldn't believe that the foolish man would have been so naïve to think that Logan wouldn't be affected by Tara's condition. Right now, she was in just as much danger from him as she was from other wolf shifters seeking her out.

Maybe even more so.

That thought sobered him fast. Logan forced the logical side of his nature to reason this out. She was a human woman, albeit almost-a-Goddess, and she was chosen to be mated to a wolf Prince. She was only a job to him. Nothing more.

They had hours, miles, to go before reaching Spokane. Chances were that they would run into wolf shifters out searching for her. He wasn't worried about protecting her because he knew he would fight to the death to keep her safe. But … who was going to protect her from him?

"You're frowning at me like this is my fault," Tara said, breaking into his dark thoughts. "I'm willing to make this easy for you and leave right now. I can disappear. You can tell Damian that you couldn't find me."

"I'm wishing that I hadn't found you," he muttered, "but I'm not about to let you just up and disappear now that I have you. I intend to take you to Damian. As quickly as possible."

"You're assuming that I'm willing to go with you."

Logan growled at her rough enough to get his point across. "Willing or not, angel, you're going to Damian."

"You'll drag me kicking and screaming every step of the way. And I don't think you want that type of attention. We certainly won't get far."

Logan studied her rebellious expression. She was such a little thing to be so tough when she needed to be. He really liked her spunk. He forced back a grin. He didn't think letting her know that he admired her bravery was a very smart thing to do right now.

Instead he decided on a different tactic. He needed to make her realize how much danger she was in right now as long as she was in heat and there were wolf shifters out there looking for her. "You're going to take off on your own, in your condition? A shifter on the prowl for a possible mate isn't something you want to have to face, Tara. Especially not alone. Without protection."

She was adorable when she blushed like now. He had the sudden urge to find out if that blush covered her whole body. His groin tightened. He groaned under his breath.

"I've been fine on my own for awhile. I don't see why it would be any different now."

"Dammit, Tara. It's completely different now. Every wolf shifter in the area is going to be able to sniff you out. You have no powers to protect yourself, not until you're mated with Damian. Do you really want to take the chance on you own?"

"I have a few magical powers. And I've been trained in the martial arts. I don't think it would be easy for someone to get to me."

"Oh yeah?" Logan felt like swearing. She was being so naïve! He wanted to shake some sense into her. "It wasn't so hard for me. And you're still here, as my captive."

"Jerk," she muttered.

"Maybe. But you're in my custody and you're not going anywhere without me. You might as well resign yourself to the fact that I'm going to deliver you—untouched—to Damian."

"Are my car keys in your pocket?"

Logan blinked rapidly in surprise at the calm question. "Why?"

"Because I'm leaving."

He didn't have time to figure out what she meant. She jumped to her feet and flew across the room at him. He didn't even have time to react. Just as she reached him she did a graceful leap into the air and her leg arched straight up at his face. The blow from her foot sent him reeling backwards.

Stunned, he started to rise and she slammed an arm into his chest, and then followed it with a kick to his ribs. He went back down again, breath lost, and pain streaking through him. He barely had time to register that her foot was aiming for his face. The blow sent his vision swirling into blackness, and his last conscious thought was that his little angel had turned into the devil himself.

Chapter Eight

Tara shoved her hand into Logan's front pocket of his jeans and fished out her car keys. She stopped for a long moment to look at his face, and a pang of guilt hit her hard. She hated doing that, but she had warned him.

She grabbed her suitcase and hurried out the hotel room to her car. A freeway sign not far from the entrance to the hotel read *Salt Lake City 25 miles.* She started to go in that direction and then changed her mind. Logan, as well as any of Damian's other people, would think she would go there and try to hide. She hadn't closed the apartment she and Mark had rented, but she figured they knew about it and would look there first. So, she turned the car in the opposite direction. Arizona, then Mexico, wasn't that far away.

Tara drove for hours, her nerves stretched to the limit, her thoughts chaotic. Just yesterday she had thought her problems with the Prophecy were over because she was now pregnant with another man's child. Instead, her entire world was turned upside down and she was running from a fate that had no intention of letting her go.

Her thoughts strayed to Logan. Had she hurt him too badly? He hadn't given her a choice. His arrogant attitude hadn't allowed for any further discussion or compromise. Instead, he'd tried to frighten her with threats of other shifters chasing her.

She wasn't that naïve to think she was completely safe on her own. Especially now that her body was in the mating cycle. But she was confident enough to think she might be able to protect herself until it was over.

Her mother hadn't told her everything. She wished she was better prepared to handle this, and knew what to expect. She was exhausted, yet an unknown urge kept her on edge and alert. It was eating away at her like a ravenous beast deep inside. She kept alternating between being hot and then cold. *Great. I'm twenty-years-old and I feel like I'm having hot flashes!*

Maybe she just needed to eat. She couldn't remember when she'd last had nourishment. As if to confirm this, her stomach growled loud and long. She maneuvered the car onto an off ramp and headed to the small truck stop off the freeway. She perused the parking lot when she parked and turned off the car. Nothing seemed out of the ordinary. There were a few trucks, and one other car. Satisfied that it was relatively safe, she got out of the car and went into the small diner.

•

Damian Sinclair sat upon the large boulder, regal and shoulders straight, as he looked down at the gathered wolf clan below him. Somewhere among them was a traitor. Or even more than one. He'd been suspicious for a long time now. And the danger kept escalating.

Yesterday's attempt on his younger brother, Colin's, life was the last straw. It was time to let the enemy know that he was aware of him. Or them, he thought as he carefully perused each wolf face.

These were his people. It was hard, having to accept that someone among those he called friends and subjects might be a threat to all he held dear.

A noticeable stir rippled among the group of wolves when a lone female sauntered into the clearing. She was smaller, more delicate, than a lot of the other females. Her brown fur was soft and shiny. She glanced at Damian before lowering her eyes in submission and going to stand with the others.

Damian knew the thoughts of the other wolves. As Prince and Alpha of the Pack, he commanded their full respect. This lone female was the only Pack member who was allowed to disobey any of his rules or commands.

She was not his mate.

But she was the love of his soul.

Damian had loved Emily Danse all their lives. But the Prophecy kept them from becoming true mates. He was destined to mate with another. But he would never love that chosen mate.

He thought briefly of Tara Stuart. She would bring great power to him and the wolf clans. He would care for her, protect her, and give her the respect she deserved.

But he would never give her his heart and soul. *Those belong to Emily. Forever.*

Still, Damian was Alpha and Prince first and foremost. The welfare of his clans came first. He would obey the Prophecy, no matter the personal cost.

That's if he lived long enough to do so. The strange illness that was spreading through his body was slowly gaining momentum. When he'd first become sick, he'd thought it only a temporary fluke. Shifters rarely got sick; their immune systems were a hundred times stronger than a human's. He'd even put it down to becoming older. He was past his prime and even though his life span would last for many more decades, his body had been through countless battles over the past century and it was starting to show the stress.

Not for the first time, he wondered at the strange malady attacking his body. Not even the healer of the Pack had been able to pin point any one reason for the illness. Damian was left to wonder if he would soon be better. Or not.

But his first priority was to deal with the traitor. His brother Colin was still recovering from the attempt on his life. He'd been out hunting when a lone wolf had attacked him, taking him by surprise. Any other time Colin could have handled the fight and won. He was a warrior only second best to Damian. But the lone wolf had outside help: a tranquilizer dart had been shot into Colin's hind leg right before the other wolf attacked. Colin hadn't stood a chance at defending himself. The lone wolf had left him for near dead, bloodied, shredded and barely breathing.

Rumors had flown among the wolf clans. Some claimed it had been a mountain lion that had attacked Colin. Damian knew better. The musky wolf smell was still lingering on his brother's body when they found him. The only problem was that it wasn't a wolf from their immediate Pack. So, that left the questions of where had he come from and who had helped him?

Damian knew there were dissenters among the clans. The Prophecy had never left any room for Free Will, and not every wolf shifter was complacent with what had been set forth as unchangeable degree from the Shifter Goddess.

There were many reigning Houses among the Clans the world over, but Damian's had been the one chosen to fulfill the Prophecy for the wolves' part. Once it had been set in motion, and he had married the half-human Goddess, Damian would then rule over the entire world of wolf shifters.

Some believed that he would also rule over all the other shifter species in the world. Since no one remembered the exact details of the ancient Prophecy, no one was sure what would occur after Damian's union with Tara.

He had every reason to suspect that the attempt on Colin's life was a warning to him. And ... that it had come from one of the other ruling Houses. But which one? Who would dare go against the Goddess Azina's decree?

Damian looked over the crowd before him. Was one of them a traitor? Could the danger be so close and he not know who it is? His sense weren't as sharp as they had been before his strange illness. What if he couldn't ferret out the traitor? Would Colin be in more danger? Damian shuddered with a new thought. What about Tara? Would he be able to protect her?

A cold chill racked his body, followed by waves of pain. It took every ounce of willpower he had to remain standing and appear unaffected by the sickness that was determined to kill him. If he showed any weakness, his power and control over the clans would be lost.

Damian straightened his shoulders and lifted his head, regal and proud. He addressed the gathered clan, making sure his voice was firm, strong and kingly.

"The attempt on Prince Colin's life is being thoroughly investigated. We will find the ones responsible and mete out dire punishment. For now, I want you all to be more than careful. I want you to be very observant. Although our clan does not deal with the human world, it still manages to intrude into our lives here. Colin's attacker had help. From a human. If you see anyone or hear anything unusual, come to me immediately."

Damian dismissed the crowd and studied them as they wandered off. He still couldn't fathom that one of their own was in any way responsible for all that was happening lately. With a sigh, he allowed his body to slump in exhaustion.

Emily sauntered up to him. "Beloved, you are tired," she said softly. She nuzzled his neck, her touch soothing and loving. "I will sit with Colin for awhile. You should rest."

"I can't rest, Em. I need to find out who is behind all this." He looked away from her, not wanting to see the pain come into her eyes at his next words. "Tara will be here in another day or two. I can not allow her to come into a danger zone and put her life at risk. Who ever this traitor is, I must find him and stop him before she arrives."

Emily touched her nose to his. "You will find him. And Tara will be safe. You are the Prince, Damian. Nothing can stand in your way."

"Ah, love," he whispered against her neck. "I wish I could be as sure as you are."

"All will be well, Damian," Emily said, her voice full of conviction and love. "I know it. What is meant to be will be."

Damian hoped she was right. But he couldn't help thinking that her words sounded more ominous than comforting.

•

Not wanting to linger any longer than she had to, Tara ate a quick meal and left the diner. It was already late evening and the parking lot was dark and almost empty. She hurried to her car. If luck stayed on her side, she could be in Arizona in another few hours.

She had left Logan semi-conscious, but the way he recovered so quickly, she was sure he hadn't remained that way long. She wondered if he was following her even now. Or had he headed to Salt Lake City? *I know I can't be so lucky to have him just forget the whole thing and not come after me.* She hadn't known him that long, but she knew his strength of will was indomitable.

When she reached her car, she belatedly thought to pull her keys out of her purse. Her delay cost her.

A strong arm came around her waist and a large hand clamped over her mouth. Tara struggled against the hard body holding her and tried to scream past the restraining hand. A rough chuckle came from her captor and she shivered in fear.

"No use in fighting, pretty lady. I just wanna be friends and talk."

Tara's heart raced. This wasn't a shifter like her first panicked thought had been. She didn't know how, but she could sense that he was a human. Probably even a rapist! Why hadn't she been more careful? She struggled harder, and kicked back with her legs and feet.

Somehow she managed to land a kick right in the man's groin. He roared and released her to clutch at his private parts. Tara used that moment to swing into attack. She arched up and landed two swift, jaw-breaking kicks straight to his face. He went down without a fight.

She spun around and fumbled to insert the key in the car door. She had to get out of here! The key slipped from her sweating hands and she dropped to the ground to search for it. "No!"

Before she even had time to cry out, strong hands reached down, clasped her waist and yanked her to her feet. She started to fight back, thinking it was the attacker. A voice, hard and deep muttered, "Tara, stop fighting me and get in the damn car!"

She stared up into Logan's enraged features. "Logan!" She couldn't believe it was him. She went weak with relief. She had the uncontrollable urge to fly into his arms. But Logan wasn't in the comforting mood. He unlocked the door, swung it open and then shoved her inside. She lost her balance as she fell onto the driver's seat, but then righted herself and moved over to the passenger side. Logan got in and slammed the door close. He jammed the key into the ignition and the car roared to life.

He pulled out of the parking lot so fast Tara uttered a protest, "My tires!" She was sure they had left tire skids all the way from the parking lot to the street leading to the freeway.

They were back on the freeway in mere minutes. Tara tried hard to calm her breathing and slow down her racing heart. She kept glancing sideways at Logan. The harsh look of rage on his face made her keep her mouth shut. She had the feeling that letting him calm down first was her smartest option.

An hour of agonizing silence later Tara couldn't stand it any more. He was still angry but they had to deal with this. He was driving way too fast ... and heading north, straight to Spokane.

"How did you find me? And so fast?"

He didn't answer right away. He didn't even glance at her. Tara chewed on her bottom lip. *Stubborn man. Just because I bested him earlier, his pride is hurt.*

"Are you going to talk to me or just pout because I beat you up and got away?"

"Dammit," Logan growled roughly. His voice was raspy with rage. "I ought to turn you over my knee and redden your butt."

He wouldn't dare! She glanced at him under lowered lashes. Would he? "I didn't really hurt you, did I?"

Logan's only answer was to growl again. The sound was ominously frightening.

Okay, maybe she should change the subject. Lesson learned. Never injure a shifter's pride. "Are we going to stop somewhere tonight? It's getting late."

Logan made a choking sound in his throat. She thought it sounded like a half-groan, half growl. "We're not stopping."

Now what was she going to do? She couldn't exactly jump from a speeding car. And besides, she wouldn't get far on foot on the freeway. She closed her eyes and did something she hadn't done in a long while. She prayed to the Goddess.

Dear Goddess Azina. I know Your will is that my part in the Prophecy be fulfilled. But I need more time. I need time to accept this. Everything is happening too fast. Please give me Your mercy in this, just this one time.

She felt guilty praying when she hadn't bothered to in so long. Would the Goddess show mercy? She didn't deserve it, but she hoped for it now with all her heart.

The Goddess answered. Her car gave a choking lurch. Logan swore a blue streak. Tara knew immediately what was wrong. They were low on gas. Too low. They would have to stop now.

"What luck," she murmured, trying not to sound too happy about it. "There's a gas station off the next exit coming up. There's a hotel, too." Logan's response wasn't nice. She looked at him, her face a mask of surprise. "Are half those foul words real words, or are you making them up as you go?"

He shot her a glare so hot, she almost cringed. "Shut up, Tara. You're pushing your luck with me, and that's not a good idea."

Tara shut her mouth. She stayed silent until they had refueled the car and then rented a room for the night. She wasn't sure why Logan had relented and decided to stop for the night but she was more than a little thankful. She was feeling so drained, she didn't think she could have gone further without rest. Only her will to get away the first chance she got again was keeping her on her feet.

She perused the room—only one bed. She was so tired, she was ready to fall into it and sleep for hours. She glanced at Logan as he brought in her suitcase and his backpack. Why hadn't he requested two beds? Granted, this one was a king-size bed ... but she was not going to share it with him!

Logan saw her staring at the bed. "Don't complain," he muttered, "This was the only room left. If you hadn't taken us so far out of the way with your little side-trip down to Arizona, we'd be closer to Washington now."

She bought some time, but not much. And he was right; it was her fault that they were now in a one-bed room for the long night ahead.

That bed was making her nervous. And she didn't like the chaotic emotions swirling inside her every time she looked at it.

Might as well get this over with. "Where are you going to sleep?" She took her suitcase from his hands and placed it in the center of the bed.

Logan stared at her for long moments. The odd gleam in his eyes as he looked at her had her heart beating way too fast. Tara grimaced. She hadn't been this nervous that first night alone with Mark. Why was Logan causing so much havoc in her? Invisible butterflies fluttered in her stomach. She broke away from his gaze and turned back to open her suitcase. She expected him to agree.

"The bed is big enough for two."

Oh! He couldn't be serious! She was too nervous to look directly at him again. "I'm not sharing a bed with a stranger." There! That sounded firm enough.

"I'm not a stranger."

His short sentences spoken in such a deep rough tone was making her nerve endings tingle with an acute sensual awareness of him. Everything about him.

"That's right," she said, putting a little sarcasm into her voice, "I've known you for over twenty-four hours now. Of course, half that time you were a cat. Hmm. You're right, there's no need for us to feel like strangers. We can sleep together and not worry about anything."

"I didn't say anything about sleeping."

Chapter Nine

"Oh." Tara's heart raced. What was he saying? Did she really want to know?

Logan sighed. She heard him grumble under his breath. She risked a glance at him and saw him run his hand through his hair as if agitated.

She couldn't stand it. This man affected her like no other man ever had. She wasn't sure why and she didn't want to reason why not. She cleared a throat gone dry. "Logan?"

"Don't look so worried, angel," he ground out roughly. "I'm not going to take advantage of you. You belong to Damian, and I'm just the delivery guy, remember?" He stomped over to a chair by the bed. Lifting it, he carried it back to the door and set it down against the door frame. "I have no intention of sleeping. Why don't you get a shower and then go to bed? We'll be leaving before dawn tomorrow."

"So early?" She hated the vulnerable sound in her question but it slipped out before she could stop herself.

"Yeah," he growled. "You caused us a delay I hadn't anticipated. The sooner I get you safely to Damian, the better."

Why did she have the feeling that his sentence seemed incomplete? Was he saying something more? Or was she just hoping? *And why the heck am I hoping for him to be a little reluctant in taking me to Damian? I must be too tired. I'm thinking crazy thoughts that I have no business thinking. Goddess, help me!*

She had to remind herself if she was noticing Logan was acting as though he was feeling anything for her, then it had to be because of her condition. She was a job to him and nothing more.

Then, why did that thought hurt so much?

Tara spent a little longer in the shower than she'd intended. By the time she got out, she felt even more drained. She blamed her exhaustion for making her forget to bring a robe into the bathroom with her. Now, she'd have to go out there—in front of Logan—wearing nothing more than a thin, silk nightdress that only reached her thighs.

She smoothed her hands down the nightgown, took a deep breath, and then walked out of the bathroom.

•

Logan dropped the cup of coffee he was holding. It hit his boots before splattering to the carpet. *Oh, man.* She took his breath away, and every coherent thought he had. His hungry gaze roamed over her every inch.

From her tousled, almost-dry hair, to the curve of her bare shoulders. To the thin straps of silk that barely held that sexy slip high enough to cover the tops of her breasts. Her nipples peaked. Logan swallowed hard. His gaze caressed over her breasts, down her tiny, flat stomach, straight to the vee of her thighs. That damn silk gown was thin enough to see that she wasn't wearing panties.

Logan was in trouble. They both were.

He muttered the foulest word he could think of. It only fueled the fire burning deep inside him. She blushed, and the fire threatened to rage out of control. His erection, which had been semi-hard since the first moment he'd met her, now reared to life, pushing against the restraint of his jeans. His entire body was rock hard.

Stand still. Don't move. Don't breathe in her scent. She doesn't belong to you. She's just a job. Don't move. He mentally repeated the mantra of words over and over.

Tara broke the spell. She made a quick dash to the bed and jumped in, pulling the covers up to block his view. He couldn't even breathe a sigh of relief. The bed wasn't the best place for her to be right now!

Lucky for them both, she was thinking clearly enough to try and dispel the hot tension in the air between them. She reached out and turned off the lamp on the bedside table, enveloping the room in semi darkness. She murmured softly, "Good night" and turned away to face the wall.

Logan stood there for a long time. He'd never expelled so much energy before to keep from doing something he so desperately wanted to do. It took every ounce of willpower he had in him.

Finally, he breathed out a deep exhale of resignation and sat down in the chair. This was going to be a long night.

•

When the first, faint sound came Logan was ready. His tense body had never relaxed, and his senses were on full alert, stretched to the limit by his mental battle of restraint over the last four hours. He immediately got up from the chair and moved it away from the door, careful not to make even the slightest sound. He glanced over at Tara and saw that she was still sleeping.

He hated the thought of bringing the battle into the room and waking her, but it was better than fighting outside and someone else witnessing it. He could only hope she would stay clear and not distract him.

He'd smelled the wolf shifter even before he'd heard that faint step near the door. His senses told him there was only one out there. The way he was feeling, he could only hope that the shifter was a worthy opponent; he needed a fight right now.

He watched the door handle turn ever-so-slightly. He'd purposely kept it unlocked, wanting the adversary to come inside for the confrontation. The door opened so slowly it was barely noticeable. Logan stepped back to allow the shifter further into the room. He waited until the shifter was fully inside and adjusted to the darkness before he spoke.

"Come in, wolf pup," he growled low. "I've been itching for a fight for hours now. Nice of you to oblige."

The wolf shifter, in man form, faced Logan. He growled roughly. "She's not mated," he stated gravelly. "I can smell it." He made another sniffing noise. "And you're a damn cat!" His hungry gaze settled on the still sleeping Tara and then turned back at Logan. "Why have you waited to claim her? She's obviously ripe and ready."

"She's off limits," Logan warned in a steely tone.

"Yeah? Well, you know as well as I do that any female in the mating cycle is fair game. Ready to fight for her, cat?"

Logan grinned and stretched, catlike and graceful. "Hey, I'm ready, anytime. It's in my nature."

They slowly started circling each other. Logan watched for any indication that the shifter would choose to fight in wolf form. He didn't care what form they used; he knew he'd wipe the floor with this measly dog. The wolf shifter must have known he'd stand a better chance fighting as a man than against Logan's lion form, so he stayed human. Yet, his movements and expressions were anything but human.

He growled and bared his teeth, staring Logan straight in the eyes in the way of wolf aggression.

Logan's adrenaline surged. This fight was just what he'd needed ever since Tara had come out of the bathroom earlier. His body craved the release from the pent-up emotions and unrelenting desire that held him in so tight a grip.

They were still circling each other and growling beneath their breaths when Tara awoke and sat up in bed with a startled "Oh!" Logan didn't break stride, but hissed at her, "Stay there."

The wolf shifter must have thought that the perfect chance to strike. He surged forward and threw a punch at Logan. Ducking, Logan swung his fist up and straight into his opponent's jaw. The sound of a cracking jaw bone was loud in the room and Tara made a little squealing noise. Logan determinedly ignored her and swung another fast punch. This one landed in the shifter's stomach.

But the shifter was bigger and more heavily muscled than Logan and he didn't go down easy. He threw his entire body into Logan, landing a solid punch straight to the gut. Both men lost their balance and fell to the floor locked in a raging battle that had fists flying, teeth sinking into skin, and ferocious growls that built in crescendo. They rolled across the floor, locked together, until they landed up against the bed. Logan was on top and he slammed his fists into the other man's face, throwing one punch after the other in rapid succession. Blood splattered and bones cracked.

From the edge of the bed, looking over at them, Tara screamed, "Stop, Logan! You're going to kill him."

Logan barely heard her, the roar of battle in his ears deafening him, and the red haze of bloodlust blinding him to all else but the exhilarating rush of victory.

It wasn't until Tara flew off the bed and rushed to his side that he even realized the shifter was unconscious and bleeding profusely. She grabbed his arm. "Logan, please stop!"

Logan drew back from the limp body beneath him. His hands were still clenched in fists, bloodied and bruised. He swallowed back the sudden roar of triumph his lion nature wanted to shout.

The primal side of his nature gloried in the bloodied mess he'd left of the shifter.

A strange sound penetrated the red haze still encompassing his senses. He slowly turned to face the woman at his side.

Tara was crying. The tears fell down her soft cheeks in rivulets as she sobbed his name over and over. He couldn't stand her crying. He would never be able to.

Logan shoved to his feet. He reached down and grabbed Tara by the shoulders, pulled her up and straight into his arms. She clung to him as he held her tight and as close as their clothes would permit. He heard himself purring as he buried his face in her soft hair.

"Shhh, angel. Don't cry. You're safe now."

Everything primal in him shouted with elation. He had protected his woman.

Whoa. Logan's body shook with sudden fear. When had his feelings changed to this ... this startling realization that he thought of her as his? Goddess, help them both.

Before he could even reason out the unwanted revelation, Tara suddenly jerked from his arms. She threw fisted punches to his chest, pounding hard and fast. He just stared in shock.

"What were you thinking? You killed him!" She cried harder. "You could have been killed too. Why didn't you just threaten him and let it go at that?"

Logan blinked several times to clear the red haze that appeared in his gaze again. He couldn't believe what she was saying.

"Threaten him?" He choked on the expletives falling out of his mouth. "Are you that naïve? What did you expect me to do? Sit down and have a civil conservation and explain to him that you belong to someone else and he couldn't claim you? Oh yeah, that would have worked. Your damn scent beckoned him here, tempting him with the knowledge that you were a female ready to mate. His animal senses were on full alert and his human side wasn't even surfacing. Yeah, talking him out of ... raping you would have been the best solution. Sorry I didn't think about it first."

Tara gasped at his words. He felt a moment of elation that he'd managed to shock her. Good. She deserved it after her accusing tirade. He'd just defended her, protected her, and she was mad because of the way he had accomplished it.

Tara angrily swiped at the tears still falling down her face. "Are you always such a bastard?"

"Ask me that after I have to kill a few more damned shifters determined to take you from me."

She looked up at him with those big blue-purple eyes wide and her mouth formed a silent O. When she finally spoke, her voice trembled. "Take me from ... you?"

He'd said it. And he meant it. That scared the hell out of him. But he wasn't going to take it back. He turned away from her and commanded roughly, "Get dressed. We're leaving."

Tara stared at him, tears and shock still apparent. "But we can't leave a dead body here!"

Logan shot her an angry glare. "He's not dead. You stopped me before I killed him. And being a shifter, he'll be conscious and on the mend in a couple of hours."

Adrenaline still surged through him. He wanted to wake the damn shifter and start the fight all over again. Do anything to get rid of the volatile emotions bombarding his senses and keeping his body on fire with a dangerous need that was slowly starting to consume his every thought.

Tara stayed where she was. He knew she was still scared. He could feel the emotion rolling off her, making her scent that much stronger in his nostrils. But he knew he was close to doing something that he shouldn't—and if she didn't stop looking at him like that—then he'd break.

He had to be harsh. It was the only way. "Stop looking so shocked, angel," he stated roughly. "This won't be the last time you see this kind of thing. There will be other shifters hunting you, and I'll have to fight them. Even kill them if necessary." He hardened his tone, "And then, after you're married to Damian, there are sure to be times when something like this happens. It's part of our world, our nature. You might as well get used to it."

"No!" Tara's face paled. She wrapped her arms around her waist and trembled. "I don't want to get used to it. I can't bear the thought of you—"

Logan's heart stuttered. His body tightened, his erection pushed hard against his jean front, and he choked back a hungry groan. He knew what she'd been about to say. He could see it in her eyes. She cared enough about him that she couldn't stand the thought of him fighting or getting hurt. He knew he shouldn't let that knowledge turn into something more. He knew he should turn away from her, right then and there. He knew it, but couldn't.

"Damn, Tara," he groaned out. "Don't say another word. Trust me on this, angel."

"Logan," she whispered his name, the sound coming out half tearful, half caressing.

Logan lost his mental battle to turn away from her. Two long strides had him in front of her. He clamped her upper arms and roughly hauled her up against him. He caught her gasp of surprise with his mouth. He took her lips in a kiss so needy, so hungry, he felt like he could devour her without ever taking another breath. Her soft mouth trembled beneath the onslaught of his hard lips but she didn't struggle. Instead she melted against him and opened her mouth to his demand.

He drank in her sweetness, and wanted more. He tangled a hand in her hair to hold her head at a better angle, to deepen the kiss, and claim every tiny inch of her hot, sweet, mouth.

She moaned into his ravaging mouth, and he groaned back. He moved his free hand down her back to the curve of her hips. When he cupped her buttock and pressed her into him, she moaned again, the sound so sexy he almost came right there.

Logan reluctantly tore his mouth from hers and stared into her bemused expression. Her blue-purple eyes were dark and filled with a mysterious light he couldn't decipher. Her red, swollen lips were parted as she gasped in short quick breaths. He almost forgot to breathe.

He wanted to kiss her again. Hell, if he was being so honest, then he had to admit he wanted a lot more than just another kiss. His erection pushed and pulsed heatedly against the fabric of his jeans and her nightdress, demanding release.

Tara felt his hardness pressed so intimately against her and her eyes suddenly widened. She tried to pull back from him but Logan couldn't force himself to let her move even an inch. Her hands were trapped between them and she slowly slid them up his chest. He felt every spot she touched like a hot caress scorching him. And he reveled in it.

But her hands didn't stop at his chest. She moved them up to cup his face. Logan saw the passion fade from her beautiful eyes and turn into something different. He stiffened, ready to stop her from saying what he could already see there in the dark depths. He wasn't ready to release her. His mind argued that he shouldn't even be touching her. But his body wasn't listening. Only craving.

"Logan," she whispered softly, the tears in her voice again. His heart lurched. "We can't do this."

"You wanted that kiss as much as I did, Tara," he stated. "And I can see it in your eyes—you want more."

"But the only reason you kissed me is because ..." She paused and blushed. He watched the soft pink color creep over her cheeks and wanted to follow the flow of it with his tongue as it covered her neck and further. "Because of my ... condition."

"Damn it all," he muttered. Was she right? Had the exalting rush of the fight and then the beckoning scent of her reaction been the catalyst to make him forget everything else?

He wanted to believe that. It would make things so much easier.

Goddess, help him. He knew why he had kissed her. And no matter how hard he tried to convince himself that it would be the only time he would ever again let his guard slip, Logan knew it wasn't true.

That thought scared the hell out of him.

Chapter Ten

The silence in the car was unbearably strained. They drove through the night, and Tara tried hard to keep from begging Logan to stop somewhere else. She knew she was only delaying the inevitable. There was no way she could prevent what was to be, and Logan was determined to get it over with as quickly as possible.

She'd never seen anyone look so angry, so dangerous, as he had when she'd stopped him from kissing her again. Not that she'd wanted to stop him. If she hadn't been thinking logically, she would have begged for more. More kisses. More of everything ...

Heat had rolled off him as though his body was on fire. His arms held her like a steel band, pressing her into the pulsing hardness of his erection. His cat eyes had gleamed with an inner light of desire, passion and lust. It was that last emotion that had sobered her instantly. In a clarifying instant she realized that the very same reason a stranger, a shifter, had broke into their room and tried to get to her was the same reason Logan was reacting to her then. Her mating cycle. The mating pheromones her body was emitting had enticed him just it had the other shifter.

She'd never felt such hurt. Why she did, she couldn't reason even to herself. But the fact that Logan had reacted that way because of something beyond either of their control hurt her deep.

It was crazy to feel that way. Logically, she knew that. But something deep inside her had ignited a need she hadn't even been aware of having until that magical, heat-filled moment when Logan had taken her in his arms and kissed her.

How could she let herself feel this way about him? Even now, hours later, her nerve endings still tingled with the memory of his passionate embrace. Even now she wanted to move closer to him and beg him to take her in his arms again.

She glanced at his hands as they clutched the steering wheel. His knuckles were bruised and still had traces of blood. She shuddered. He'd nearly killed that man. If she hadn't been able to stop him …

Tara bit back a groan. *I might as well admit that some small part of me gloried in his fight to protect me. How sick is that?* She had to remember that he was only doing his job.

A small voice whispered deep inside her, *Yeah, but that kiss had nothing to do with his job.*

When they'd both suddenly come to their senses, Logan had shoved her away from him curtly telling her to get dressed. He'd stomped from the room, taking his backpack to the car. Her heart was racing so fast she felt breathless as she grabbed a clean pair of jeans and a blouse and hurried to the bathroom to change. As she dressed she tried to calm down, but her body felt too warm, too over-stimulated.

When she'd come out of the bathroom, Logan was standing at the door waiting impatiently for her to repack her nightdress. He grabbed the suitcase as soon as she closed it and then stomped back out. She followed … after one last glance at the still-unconscious shifter on the floor.

One look at Logan's harsh, uncompromising features and she knew better to try and talk to him. They drove in silence like that for hours. The palpable tension within the small confines of the car grated on her already-stretched nerves.

The green freeway sign said *Entering Washington*, and Tara's heart stuttered with dread. So close. A pre-dawn sky heralded a new day. The first day of the rest of her life.

She was going to be handed over to a wolf shifter and married to him as soon as possible in order to fulfill a Prophecy that had been made centuries before her birth. She was going to become a reigning monarch over the Wolf Clans. Everything that had once been Tara Stuart was going to be lost as she was thrown into the role of Queen to a species that was less human than she was.

Panic surged deep inside her, nausea rolling in its wake. She clutched at her stomach. Before she could stop herself, she blurted out, "I can't do this."

I can't! This is crazy! She didn't even realize she'd grabbed the door handle until Logan growled, "Don't do it, Tara. Take your hand off that handle. Now."

She placed her folded hands in her lap, clasped them tight together, and took a deep breath. Her whole body shook from the force of holding back her growing panic.

"Talk to me," she pleaded desperately. "Please. Tell me everything is going to be alright. Tell me my whole life isn't about to change into some strange nightmare I can't wake from, ever. Tell me, Logan, please."

Logan maneuvered the car onto an exit. At the crossroads, he turned left and drove another few miles. Tara was confused. Why were they going off and away from the freeway now? Logan hadn't answered her, and the silence in the car made her want to scream. Was he still angry that she'd stopped him earlier from doing something that they both knew was wrong? Didn't he have the least bit of compassion in him to say something, anything?

She looked out the window and caught the sign that read *Mills Crossing 2 miles*. Where were they going? Wasn't Mills Crossing just a drive-through town with a few buildings? It was a favorite campground for tourists who enjoyed the authentic cabin rentals and privacy of the area. She'd visited there once as a child. Her father had taken Jason fishing while she, Mara and their mother had driven the hour back into the nearest town to shop.

Half an hour later, Logan turned the car onto a dirt road. She could tell it was a private entrance, and most likely would lead to one of the many cabins near the lake.

Her guess was confirmed when they pulled up in front of a large log cabin and Logan stopped the car. He turned off the car lights and looked over his shoulder at the road behind them. If at all possible, he seemed even more tense than before.

"Logan?"

He didn't look at her. Instead he muttered, "Go inside, Tara. The key to the front door is under the flower pot on the right step. Wait for me inside, but don't turn on the lights."

She wanted to ask why. She wanted to demand to know what was going on. But one look at his features and she changed her mind. She got out of the car and hurried to the front door. She found the key, unlocked the door, and went inside. When she turned to close the door behind her she gasped in shock.

Logan had changed into his mountain lion form and was slinking off into the surrounding woods.

Tara slammed the door close and locked it. What was going on? Uneasy and confused, she moved carefully into the dark interior of the cabin. Logan had told her not to turn the lights on, but luckily she had great night vision and was able to maneuver around the furniture without bumping into anything, until she finally came to the sofa that sat against the wide, picture window.

She noted instantly that the window was coated with a shimmering texture that she knew was used for blocking anyone from looking in from the outside. Her father had used the same security coat for their home windows in Scotland but hadn't seen the need for it in the isolated area of Grant.

After staring intently out the window into the still-early morn darkness she couldn't see anything moving, and wondered where Logan had gone and why. The cabin was chilly and she got up from the window seat to search for firewood. She found a small, neat stack by the fireplace and was relieved she wouldn't have to go outside to look for any. After checking to make sure the fireplace was ready for use, it only took a few minutes to have a warm, roaring fire blazing. She sat down on the soft, flat cushions in front of the fireplace and hugged her knees to her chest. The firelight lit up the room and she looked around.

It was a lovely room—very cabin-authentic with its dark logs and architect. The furniture was a mixture of dark brown leather and wood, and the walls were adorned with various paintings with Old West themes. The flooring was wood and a few colorful Indian rugs covered the floor in spots. To the left of the front entry was a wooden staircase that curved up like a spiral, leading to the upstairs loft. To the right a set of wooden swinging doors led into another room and she assumed it was the kitchen.

Her stomach grumbled. When was the last time she had eaten anything? She glanced at her wristwatch. It was early morning, just after seven now. She frowned as she glanced toward the front door. Where was Logan? He'd been gone for a long while now, and it was really wearing on her nerves. She decided to check the kitchen for any food.

Inside the efficient little kitchen she found can goods in the cupboards, and all the cooking utensils she would need. She wasn't too enthusiastic about the choice of food but couldn't be picky right now. Her stomach was grumbling so loud she wondered if it could be heard outside.

She opened a can of hash, shredded corn beef and potatoes. She lit the gas oven after checking to make sure it was working safely. Mixing the ingredients together, she poured them into a large frying pan. While that was simmering, she searched the cupboards for ingredients to make bread. She couldn't find everything she needed but did locate a quick-mix for cornbread.

She was just turning off the oven and stove when she heard the faint sound of the front door opening. Her heart raced. Was it Logan? Or ... was it someone else?

Tara quietly pulled open the silverware drawer and grabbed a large butcher knife. If it was another shifter, she would have to defend herself the best way she could. She'd seen what it took to beat that last shifter unconscious. If Logan hadn't been the better opponent, the battle would have turned out different. It made her realize just how strong shifters were, even in their human forms.

She debated on waiting for the intruder to come to her, or for her to go out and meet him. She clutched the knife tighter in her sweaty palm as she heard the footsteps approach the kitchen. *Logan, where are you? I need you.*

The swinging doors to the kitchen slowly moved apart and Tara braced herself against the counter, raising the knife high in a defensive stance.

Logan walked into the room. She was never more relieved to see his handsome face! She dropped the knife on the counter and then—without even considering the consequences—she ran into his arms.

•

Logan caught her up in his arms with a harsh groan tearing from him. He hadn't expected her to react that way, and he wasn't prepared for what it did to him.

He'd spent the last couple of hours roaming the woods in his lion form, determined to run the relentless need raging inside him out of his system. He'd run for miles, trying desperately to keep his thoughts in cat form. When exhaustion finally made him slow down and he realized just how far he was from the cabin, he'd reluctantly turned around and came back.

Though the run in cat form had physically tired him, Logan

wasn't fortunate enough to have it benefit his chaotic mind any. And as soon as he'd transformed back into a man and had walked toward the cabin, his body wasn't so tired after all. The hard erection he'd had since kissing Tara earlier was still raging, and the need to assuage the fire inside him was growing with every step he took closer to her. He'd called himself every kind of foul name he could think of and it hadn't helped his conscience any.

He wanted her. Desperately.

She belonged to another man.

By the time he'd stepped into the cabin and got a whiff of the food she was cooking, he had made up his mind that his self discipline was going to remain strong.

As long as she helped ... by staying her distance from him.

And she'd flown into his arms the moment he'd stepped into the room. Damn, damn, damn! They were both fools and he had no idea how he was going to handle this.

He pushed her back from him. He had to stay strong. "Something smells good." He knew his voice sounded toneless, but he couldn't afford to show any emotions around her right then.

"Breakfast," she answered. After taking a long look at him, Tara turned back to the cupboard. She pulled out a set of plates and silverware and set the table for two. Logan watched her every move. Even though she was obviously tired, she moved gracefully and in an unknowingly sensual way that had his body tightening even more. There was just something incredibly special about this woman that he couldn't ignore no matter how much he wanted to.

They ate in silence. Logan knew Tara wanted to know where he'd disappeared to, but he couldn't tell her. *Hell, the last thing she needs to hear is that I had to run away from her for awhile to get control of myself.*

Tara waited until she had cleaned the kitchen before turning back to Logan who sat at the table watching her with hungry thoughts. Finally she broke the silence.

"Where are we? I know we're in Washington, in the Mills Crossing area. But ... is this where Damian lives, too?"

He distinctively heard the vulnerable, sad tone in her question. It hit him like a punch to the gut. He just prayed she wouldn't start crying—he was a goner for sure if she did.

"Damian's home is in Riverside Park. We have several hours

before we get there."

"Why did we come here, then?"

How the hell did he answer that? *I was about to explode with the need to claim you as my own, so I thought it best if I left you safely here and ran away for awhile. Yeah, that would be the smart answer! Not.* He shook his head. Right now Riverside Park seemed like a lifetime away.

"You needed a break," he finally answered. "I needed to run for awhile. This is my family cabin, so I knew you'd be safe while I was gone."

"Oh." She came back to sit at the table with him. "It's a lovely cabin. I haven't seen the upstairs, but the downstairs is so cozy, so western-authentic."

"My family's weird sense of humor," Logan told her. When she raised her brows in question, he explained, "They thought it funny that a shifter family would own a cabin in the middle of an area humans use for camping and hunting. It was like throwing the obvious into their faces: we're animals and we own this land, too."

Tara folded her hands on the table. The casual gesture didn't fool him. She was full of questions and he wondered just where those questions might eventually lead to. Just this close to her, with a table separating them, and he felt ready to jump across the table and take her right there and then. He clenched his own hands into tight fists.

"Is it difficult being a shifter in a human world?"

It wasn't the question he'd expected. "Not really. We blend in, and we're in our human forms most of the time. We own businesses, have regular home lives, families, children that go to human schools."

"Are the children able to control their shifting abilities then, at any age?"

"A shifter child usually doesn't start shifting until he is in his teens. By then, we've trained them on what to expect and what to do. They're fully prepared to keep the human world from ever discovering their secret."

Logan searched her features. What exactly was she asking? He got his answer when she abruptly asked,

"Is it possible for shifters to have children with anyone else who isn't a shifter?"

Oh man. This wasn't a discussion he wanted to talk about. Having children meant having sex first. Mating in the most intimate way. And the last thing he needed to be thinking about was that right now.

He cleared his throat. "There are half breeds. Some shifters have chosen to mate with a human and have children. The offspring have a few limitations that a normal full-blooded shifter wouldn't, but for the most part they are shifters and live in that world foremost."

"How old is Damian?"

Logan looked at her, startled with the question. "I don't know. Why?"

She looked uncomfortable. He held his breath hoping that she wouldn't suddenly blush. Every time she did he got this incredible urge to kiss every inch of silky soft skin that enticing blush touched. If circumstances had been different, if they had met under a different situation, he would have willingly given into that urge and hoped it touched every inch of her body. That mental picture pulled a groan from deep inside him.

"I just wondered," she paused, looked away from him, and nervously clasped and unclasped her hands, "if he is young enough to want ... children. I never actually thought about it, until now. Maybe he thinks my Goddess powers and his shifter blood will produce a child of uniqueness?"

Logan couldn't take much more of this conversation. The thought of Tara mating with another man and having his child wasn't something he wanted to dwell on.

"Why don't you go upstairs to the bedroom and rest for awhile," he suggested. "We can leave by late afternoon and reach Riverside Park by this evening."

He knew he was stalling the inevitable just as she'd tried from the start. He argued with himself that it was just because she was looking so fragile and exhausted ... and frightened that he wanted to make things as easy as possible for her. Once he delivered her to Damian, she was no longer his responsibility.

"I'm tired, but I don't want to sleep," she answered softly. "I know it's crazy, and I know you think I'm just trying to delay our getting to Damian. Maybe that's true. But, I don't want to sleep away the last few hours of my ... freedom." She suddenly stood up. "Can we take a walk in the woods? Maybe to the Lake?" She wouldn't even look at him. "If you're too tired after your long run, then maybe I can just go by myself. I promise I won't go too far. Or try to escape."

•

Logan was silent for long moments and Tara realized she was holding her breath. Would he believe her and trust her not to run away? She sighed. *Would I try? Would it be worth the effort?* She didn't have an answer for that. Right now her mind was telling her to get away from Logan, but her body was telling her to stay with him every last minute they were going to have before reaching Damian.

"I have no reason to trust you, angel," he answered. "But I want to. I know you can't get too far without me being able to track you down. And I've already scouted the area for any other shifters. It's relatively safe. So, if you will look me in the eyes and promise to only take a short distance walk, I'll agree to it."

Her heart sang. He was going to trust her! She didn't hesitate and she looked him straight in the eyes. "I promise."

Logan shook his head and muttered, "I must be crazy. Don't make me regret this, Tara. Be back here within the hour. If I have to come find you, then ..."

Tara couldn't help it, she grinned mischievously at him. "Then, you'll do what you wanted to do last night and 'redden my butt,' right?"

"Go," he growled. "Before I change my mind."

She smiled sweetly at him and then hurried from the room. She wasn't about to give him time to change his mind. She needed this respite.

Away from the too-closeness of the cabin.

Away from him.

Chapter Eleven

The early morning air was crisp and fresh. She breathed in and felt the tension in her body slowly fade. The surrounding woods looked so inviting. She'd roamed the area when she was a child visiting with her parents but she wasn't familiar with it now. Still, she had grown up in the wilds of Scotland and knew she wouldn't get lost here in a small wooded area.

She wandered into the cool interior of woods. The place seemed alive with small animals, beautiful green fauna, tall, thick-trunk trees with branches swaying gently. It was completely serene.

Why can't we just stay here? It was a stupid question and she chewed on her bottom lip biting down hard. It was stupid of her to want something she knew was completely out of her reach. Staying here would mean forfeiting her destined life as Queen by Damian's side. Staying here would mean …

Being with Logan.

She couldn't deny it any longer. Her feelings for the enigmatic shifter were deep. She wasn't sure when it had happened, but knew the truth was there all along. No other man had ever affected her this way. He made her feel things she had only dreamed about experiencing. His protectiveness was exciting, especially when she could sense a hint of possessiveness mixed with it.

And the hungry way he had kissed her. That memory would stay with her for the rest of her life. The thought of Damian kissing her made her suddenly sick to her stomach. How could she ever allow another man to even touch her after she'd experienced what it felt like to be in Logan's embrace?

No! She didn't want to think about it. She couldn't bear the thought. She forced the unbearable ache away and cleared her mind. There was no changing what was to be. She had learned that the hard way.

Tara let the serenity of the woods sink into her consciousness and she walked until she became too tired. It was then she realized that she had been gone long enough and that the hour Logan had given her was almost over.

Great! He'll come looking for me if I'm late, and he'll be angry when he finds me. She hated his anger. It held the unspoken promise of leading into something more ... physical. She knew he would never hurt her, not in that way, but she also instinctively knew that the physical part would be something neither of them would come out of unscathed.

A twig snapped loudly. She jumped and swung around in the direction it had come from. Was it an animal? Or Logan? Or ... another shifter?

She hated this fear. In a way, it would be a relief to finally be mated with Damian and get this chase over with.

"Logan?"

No answer. She immediately noticed that everything around her was eerily quiet, still. She didn't have a shifter's preternatural abilities to sense or smell another's presence, so she had to rely solely on her own intuition. And it was telling her that who ever was hiding near by definitely wasn't Logan.

"Who's there?" She forced her voice to stay calm. "You might as well show yourself."

Another twig snapped. This time she could tell exactly where it had come from. Yards off, to her right, was a thick set of shrubs. Tara gauged the distance she would have to run to get safely out of the woods. Logan waited, and if she knew him as well as she was beginning to then she could expect him to be pacing the edge of the woods impatiently waiting for her to return.

She took one step in the direction of safety. She stopped when she heard the slight groan. There was someone in those bushes, and possibly hurt. She couldn't walk away. She knew it was dangerous to risk, especially if it turned out that another shifter was lying in wait for her. After all she'd been through in the past few days, she still couldn't force herself to walk away from anyone—or anything that might need her help.

Tara approached the shrubs with extreme caution and her heart beating in fast trepidation. She drudged up enough calm to make her feet move. *If there's another cat on the other side of these bushes I'm going to run screaming as fast and as far as I can get. No sense in going through that situation again!* One Logan was all she could handle.

"I won't hurt you, so don't be afraid," she called out gently. *Okay, here goes.* She stepped in through the bushes and found herself in a tiny clearing, much like a nesting spot for a large animal.

And it was definitely an animal she found. Or, make that a shifter, not an animal. She didn't know how she knew it, but she was sure the dark grey wolf was not a normal animal.

Maybe it was the intelligence in his eyes. Or the way he faced her with such bravery despite the fact that his front right paw was stuck in a small animal trap and bleeding profusely.

She assessed the situation quickly. She'd seen what those kind of traps could do, and had been taught how to spring them. She met the wolf's gaze. She hoped he was sane enough to let her try and help him.

"I can spring the trap," she explained in a slow, careful tone. "It will hurt, but not for long. You just have to promise me you won't bite me." She made sure her gaze was locked with his, and hoped that her sincerity was evident. "Is that a deal?'

The wolf's gaze was hard, leery. Tara knew he was probably a shifter to be reckoned with in normal circumstances. After a few tense moments he slowly nodded his head in an all-too-human action of agreement. Tara breathed a sigh of relief.

She slowly sank to the ground and was level with his face. She examined the bleeding paw and her heart lurched. The trap had done some serious damage, and it was obvious the wolf had tried to chew his way out of it, too. She cringed, hating the sight of blood. She'd seen enough of it in the past twenty-four hours to last her a lifetime.

"As soon as I spring this lock, we'll have to get a compression on that wound immediately. Hold still."

She ran her hands over the trap and then positioned her fingers on the lock. Her father had taught her how to unlock the spring on these contraptions when she was a very young child, and she was grateful that she remembered the instructions now.

The lock sprung open with a loud popping noise. The wolf

slumped down as she carefully pulled his paw free. She cautioned him again, "Stay still, now. We need to get this bandaged."

The only thing she had available was her blouse. She hesitated for a moment. This was a shifter—a half human man. Taking her blouse off to shred it for bandages wasn't her best idea. If it was just an animal. She sighed. She really had no choice.

She glared at him in warning. "Be a gentleman and don't look. I'm going to use my blouse for a bandage. Don't make me regret helping you."

She blinked and stared at him startled. Did he actually smile? She had to look twice at the odd uplifting of his canine lips before she could decide that it was really a smile and not a snarl.

For once she was wearing a bra beneath her blouse. She had a bad habit of not wearing one when she didn't think it necessary. *Of course, I'm wearing one of my sexy bras. I couldn't have chosen a more decent one?* In her defense, she hadn't thought much about her clothes when she'd left home so abruptly.

She pulled off her blouse and gave it a hard yank to tear the sleeve. It was thin camisole and tore easily. She just hoped it was thick enough to help stop some of the bleeding. After making several long strips and then shorter ones, she carefully wrapped the wolf's paw. He winced, once, but it was so slight she almost didn't catch it. She quickly apologized, "I'm sorry."

When she finished wrapping the wound she tied a few narrow strips around it and tied them in a secure knot. "There. That should hold it."

She put her sleeveless blouse back on and then sat back and stared at him. "I know you're a shifter. Why didn't you change back into a man when you caught your paw in the trap? You might have had better luck getting it out."

"That's because shifters can't change when they're wounded."

Tara jumped, squealing in surprise at Logan's voice behind her. "Logan, you scared me!"

"Wait until later. I've got more planned," he threatened smoothly. "What the hell are you doing here with a shifter? Are you out of your lovely head?"

"He was hurt," Tara stated. "And if you remember, I can't let a wounded animal suffer if there's some way I can help."

Logan shoved her behind him. "We're going to have to talk about that careless habit. Go back to the house. I'll deal with this."

Tara heard the steely tone in his voice. She didn't like the way he said he'd *deal* with it. "Don't you dare hurt him," she warned. "He's already wounded, and he wasn't threatening me in any way."

"It's pretty obvious he can't harm you in his condition," Logan bit out through clenched teeth, a jaw muscle jumping erratically. "I'm the one you should be afraid of right now."

"I am," she answered honestly. "I'm afraid you're going to do something to him."

Tara looked down at the slumped wolf who, although was licking at the bandage, was also obviously listening to their heated exchange. She couldn't believe Logan would be so cruel as to hurt an already wounded animal. That was taking his protectiveness just too far! She wasn't going to let him do it. She pushed aside his restraining hand and moved around to stand between him and the wolf. She put her hands on her hips.

"We're taking him back to the cabin and we're going to get him back on his feet. You are not going to hurt him."

"Think again," Logan muttered.

"Logan, this is cruel. Why would you want to hurt something that hasn't hurt you?"

His brows rose in surprise. "Why? Tara, you're driving me crazy. I don't envy Damian having to control that impulsive nature of yours. You're sure to give him hell every time."

"Maybe Damian would be more compassionate."

Oh no. That wasn't the right thing to say. Dangerous storm clouds were less threatening than the look on his face now. Behind her the wolf suddenly growled low.

"Go. Back. To. The. Cabin."

Tara didn't consider herself a coward. But the clipped, rough tone of Logan's voice was frightening. She glanced back at the wolf and whispered, "I'm sorry." And then turned and hurried away. She mentally chastised herself for being so weak and hated that it was true. She really was a coward.

And in that moment she was sure she hated Logan Cross.

Chapter Twelve

She ran as fast as she could to avoid hearing what might be happening behind her. She didn't stop running until she reached the safety of the cabin. She was breathless and exhausted when she collapsed in a chair in the living room. Tears stung her eyes. But she refused to cry. She'd done enough of that for weeks now, and she wasn't sure she had many more tears left inside her.

A half an hour later, she heard Logan's footsteps outside the door. She slowly stood up and waited for him to come inside. She didn't know what she was going to say to him, but they needed to get things cleared up. Now.

Logan walked in. Behind him was a young woman. Tara gasped in surprise. She looked to be in her early twenties, and her black hair was waist length, curling over a slim body. She had large brown eyes that stared at Tara with awe.

Awe? Huh? Tara looked from the woman to Logan and then back again. Logan looked …

He looked exhausted. Tara wasn't sure what to think of that. And who was the woman standing next to him?

"This is Senya. She is mate to the shifter you helped. I told her we would give them a few supplies."

Tara knew her mouth was open. She was in shock. Was this the same Logan she had just left, angry and ready to kill again?

Something melted in her, then. The thin barrier of protection she'd mentally erected to keep her heart safe from Logan now disappeared. She felt in that moment that she knew everything there was to know about him. It was a startling revelation that touched that hidden spot deep in her soul.

She avoided his gaze and smiled at Senya. "Of course. There's plenty of food in the pantry, and I can find something for more bandages."

Logan headed to the kitchen. "I'll pack some boxes of food," he said over his shoulders. "And you can find first aid supplies upstairs in the loft's bathroom."

Tara smiled reassuringly at Senya who was still staring at her in that worshipping awestruck way and then hurried up the spiral staircase to the loft. Her heart sang with joy that events had turned out much different from what she had feared they would. Logan hadn't hurt the shifter. Instead, he was willing to help him and his mate. She grinned. *He has a compassionate heart whether he wants to admit it or not.*

She packed the first aid supplies in a basket she found under the sink. She discovered a sufficient supply of towels and washcloths in the linen closet and grabbed a few to stuff in the basket, too.

When she came back downstairs Logan was sitting a large box by the door. He turned to watch her descending the stairs and she was hard pressed to read what he was thinking. His cat eyes were dark, stormy. Yet, there was something else shining in the depths. Something that made her heart race all over again. When he looked at her that way she wanted to forget the rest of the world and what tomorrow would bring.

Senya was standing by the door, her head bowed. Tara felt awkward with the young woman's shyness. She wanted to put her at ease. "I hope this is enough to help," she told her.

Senya nodded and smiled shyly. "Yes. Thank you." She walked over to Tara and took her hands in hers. "I owe you a life-debt and I will never forget it. Your kindness and compassion will never be forgotten, either."

Tara shook her head. "You don't owe me anything. I'm just glad I could help."

"Our Prince will have a worthy mate to reign at his side," Senya said. "Our people are blessed."

Tara felt embarrassed heat flood over her cheeks. Behind Senya she heard Logan groan. *Why does he do that every time I blush? It's not his body that heats up like a miniature fire every time.*

Senya tightened her hands around Tara's for a brief moment and then whispered, "Goodbye. We will meet again, Tara Stuart."

Logan didn't look at Tara as he lifted the large box in his arms and Senya took the basket. "I'll carry this for her, and then be back soon. Stay in the cabin, and keep the doors locked."

Tara couldn't help it—she just had to say it, "Yes, sir."

She heard his growl even over Senya's loud gasp. She stifled a giggle. Laughing at him wouldn't be a smart move right now, she was sure of that.

Her heart was light when she went back into the living room to sit by the fireplace. The flames had died down from earlier but there was just enough warmth emanating to make the room comfortable and cozy.

She suddenly realized just how tired she was. She wasn't sure how long Logan would be gone but she decided that a little nap was what she needed to re-energize before he returned.

There were things they had to talk about.

Tara curled up on the floor cushions and closed her eyes. The last fleeting image in her conscious state was that of Logan's odd expression when he'd left with Senya.

•

The flames in the fireplace suddenly burst into new life, roaring high and hot. Tara gasped and woke. She felt a bit disoriented for a moment before she realized where she was. Stunned, she stared at the fire and wondered how it had managed to come back to ferocious life again.

Then she heard the heavy breathing.

She gasped and swung around to search the room. It was dark. How long had she been asleep? Where was Logan?

And who was here with her now?

"Logan? Is that you?" She instinctively knew it wasn't; she was always able to sense when he was near. The breathing became rougher. A tremble of alarm raced through her. "Who's there?"

A low, gravelly voice answered from the dark area near the stairs, "I am your destiny. You are to be my mate."

Everything inside her screamed with fear. No! She couldn't believe this was happening again. Another shifter trying to claim her! *Logan, where are you?*

She tried to calm down. She had to think clearly if she was going to get out of this safely and untouched. "Who are you? What is your name? Why are you hiding in the shadows?"

A huge, dark form slowly came forward from the darkness. Tara knew instantly it was a wolf. She'd never seen one so big before. Before she could grasp that his size was so immense, he suddenly started shifting. Within moments he was in human form.

A tall, dark haired man. Regal. And completely naked.

Tara gasped. "Damian." She didn't know how she knew but she didn't doubt it.

He nodded his head in acknowledgement. "I have come to claim you, Tara."

She stood up, her legs shaky. "You can't be here. You're supposed to be waiting for Logan to bring me to you."

"Time is running out," he answered. "You have run from me for so long. Everything has been delayed because of your fear, and your impulsiveness to deny fate."

Anger surged in her from his words. "I should have free will just like anyone else. I did what I had to do in order to remain free."

"You may have caused the loss of many lives in doing so."

"What are you talking about?" How could she have caused any deaths?

"You can not change destiny, Tara. We have to mate now. It is imperative that my reign over the world's Packs be established now."

Tara shook her head. This wasn't happening. She wanted to run. She wanted to call out for Logan. Where was he? He was always there to protect her. She needed him.

All she could do was deny the inevitable. "No. I don't want this. I can't belong to you, Damian. We can't be together, no matter what the fates say."

"The choice has been taken from you, Tara." Damian advanced on her, his glide predatory and smooth. "Come to me. Now."

"No." She had never felt such fear. But she realized that it wasn't only fear making her reject Damian. It was something more— deeper, stronger. Something she wanted to deny with every fiber of her being.

Her heart, her body, her soul … belonged to someone else.

Damian suddenly lunged at her. Tara screamed as his arms clasped her tight against him and he repelled her struggles with ease. She screamed and kicked, over and over.

"No! Logan, help me! Logan, I need you! Where are you?"

"I'm right here, angel."

The soft comforting words woke Tara from the nightmare. She opened tear filled eyes to stare directly into Logan's blue gaze. He was holding her cuddled in his arms and looking down at her with an expression she was afraid to try and fathom.

"It was a dream," she murmured in relief.

"Do you want to talk about it?"

She shook her head. She'd rather never have to think about it again. But the reality was that she was about to face the real-time moments of that dream as soon as she was delivered to Damian. No! She couldn't bear the thought! "Please, Logan, just hold me for awhile. I don't want to think about anything right now."

Logan shifted her in his arms, arranging her across his lap as he leaned back against a chair. He sighed. The sound was weary. Tara lifted her head and looked into his eyes.

What she saw there stunned her. Though his sigh had sounded tired, there was a burning brightness in his eyes. A blaze that lit the depths to fire. She caught her breath. He looked the same way when he had kissed her.

"Logan?" Her voice caught on a catchy intake of breath. The fire in his eyes gleamed hungrily and it lit a matching flame deep within her body and soul.

"Don't say anything," he muttered. "Just close your eyes and rest for awhile." He closed his own eyes for a moment. "We have to leave soon."

The words were out before she could stop them. "I want to stay here. With you."

Logan groaned. He stared into her eyes. "Tara, don't make this any harder than it already is. Nothing can change what must be."

Tara wasn't sure what he was saying but a heart-aching heaviness settled in her heart as realization hit. If he felt anything for her then he wouldn't be so willing to let Fate control what was to come.

She hated herself. She had fallen in love with Logan. No matter how much she wanted to deny it, she couldn't. But, he didn't love her. She had to accept that. She had to accept that she belonged to another man.

No! I don't want to be with anyone else. She had to make him understand that. "We're both cowards," she whispered and then hid her face against his chest. "I don't want to face my destiny. And you don't want to have anything to do with me that would cause you to dishonor your vow to Damian."

"I owe him a life-debt," Logan stated harshly. "I will honor that, no matter what."

Senya had said almost the same words. Tara wondered why it was so important to the shifters. "What does that mean, exactly? Senya said she owed me, too, and I didn't understand."

"You saved her mate's life."

"I only rescued him from the trap."

Logan shifted, holding her a little closer. "Although it was a man-made trap, it had been set by a shifter. Erik's pack has many enemies in this area. He sides with Damian's claim to rule the Packs and those opposing have tried to eliminate the supporters. When Erik was caught in the trap, Senya tried to make it back to their pack for help. They live in a small area near the lake, isolated, but not well protected. Senya couldn't get through a shifter barrier—several shifter hunters out looking for anyone who might have fallen into their traps—and she had to return to Erik without help. When she returned, you were coaxing Erik into accepting your help. She almost attacked you."

"I didn't even know she was there." She wished she had some of those preternatural senses the shifters had. It would come in handy, she was sure.

"I know." He growled under his breath. "You're like this innocent little lamb so clueless to the danger around you when you have something on your mind other than your own safety."

"And that's a bad fault?" Why did his words have to hurt?

"No." He was silent for long moments. "It's actually a very endearing trait, but it drives me crazy. I have to fight the urge to shake some sense into you. Then, I have to fight the urge to—"

Tara's heart stopped. She caught her breath. What was he saying? Was it possible that he did care about her? She raised her head from his chest and found her gaze snared with his. It took her breath away all over again.

"Damn, this is insane. I don't want to feel this way, Tara. I can't."

"What way?" *Please tell me you feel the same way I do, Logan.*

He hissed between his teeth. "Feeling like I can't breathe with wanting something that doesn't belong to me. Feeling like I could just give into my basic animal nature and take what I so desperately want and damn the consequences later."

He tightened his arms around her. "Feeling like dishonoring everything I believe in. Losing all respect I have for myself and what others have of me. Destroying a destiny that I have no right interfering in. I want to do all that, and more. For you."

Chapter Thirteen

Her heart screamed out, "Then please do it!" But her logical mind wouldn't let her say the words aloud. She couldn't bear the thought that she would be the cause of his downfall. Hadn't her own life been changed by something she couldn't control?

As much as she wanted him to love her, she didn't want to know that he would hate himself later. And she wouldn't be able to live with herself knowing that she had caused Logan to hate her …

She made up her mind. For both their sakes, she had to be strong. "We can leave now," she whispered. "There's no reason to delay any more. I know you want to deliver me to Damian as soon as possible."

"Hell." He muttered a few more foul words. He released her from his arms and set her off his lap. He surged to his feet. Tara stared up at him, frightened and elated at the same time at the fierce, hungry look in his eyes.

"I promised you time to rest before we finish the last leg of the journey. And I intend to keep that promise."

He bent down and scooped her straight up into his arms like she weighed nothing at all. Tara automatically put her arms around his neck. She looked at him, questions burning to be asked.

"I'm a shifter, angel. I don't have frail human faults. I am Prince of the largest Cat Clan in the world. If I can't be strong enough to walk away from temptation, then I'm not worthy of anything."

She admired his strength. But his will to deny whatever it was between them hurt her deeply. She closed her eyes and dropped her head on his shoulder as he carried her from the room. Not for anything would she show just how much his words hurt. She would be strong, too. Even if it destroyed her.

Logan carried her up the winding stairs and into the bedroom loft. He crossed the room slowly to the large bed. He placed Tara down on the comforter-covered bed and then stepped back to look down at her. His eyes burned with a searing fire that he couldn't hide no matter what his words said. She wanted to hold up her arms and beg him to stay with her, here in this bed. Forever.

"Sleep for awhile, angel," he murmured roughly. "We'll leave in a few hours."

Tara closed her eyes against the hunger that shone in his. She turned away from him. A few moments later she heard him leave the room. The sigh that escaped her then was heart felt and soul deep. She whispered his name, "Logan."

•

She only meant to sleep for a few minutes but it was almost an hour later when she finally woke.

She woke refreshed. And determined. She had followed her heart all her life and had done whatever it took to seek out her heart's desire despite the interference from others. She wasn't about to stop doing that now. She still had time.

Tara looked around the room and realized that because of all that had happened Logan had forgotten to bring in her suitcase from the car. Perfect.

She undressed, dropping the remaining part of her torn blouse, bra, panties and jeans to the floor in a trail that led straight to the bathroom. If that didn't get Logan's attention then nothing would!

She turned the shower on to a low stream and then stepped inside, closing the stall door. The warm water cascaded down over her in gentle torrents, easing all the aches and dissipating all the weariness from her body.

She lathered her body with the sweet smelling bar of soap she'd found with the other toiletries in the cabinet. It reminded her of a fresh, green forest after a cleansing rain.

She took her time bathing, trying hard to relax. She couldn't believe that she was even considering doing this. Logan had made it very clear that he wasn't going to compromise his morals. Was she wrong to want this? To want to have this time with him before she was wed to Damian and her entire life changed? Goddess, help them both if this was so wrong.

Before she could talk herself out of it, she turned off the shower and stepped out. She wrapped the long bath towel around her body, took a deep fortifying breath, and then left the bathroom.

She stopped, uttering a small, "Oh."

Logan stood in the center of the room holding her panties in his hands. When he raised his gaze to look at her, Tara felt that look like a searing, burning caress that touched every over-sensitive inch on her body. Her stomach fluttered with invisible butterflies. This is what she wanted, but now she was feeling nervous about the decision. Her conscience demanded to know: could she handle the consequences of what would be if she followed through on this?

Her heart answered for her. *Yes.*

Because nothing else mattered right now. She would have tonight to remember for the rest of her life. That would carry her through.

Her gaze stayed locked with Logan's hot one for long breathless moments. That hungry look burning in his blue eyes was so intense she was sure it would scorch her if she didn't break away now.

"What the hell are you doing, Tara?" Logan's voice was rough, barely above a heated whisper.

"I was taking a shower." Okay, that was stating the obvious! She just hoped she didn't blush and give away her guilt.

"You're playing with fire, and you know it," he stated harshly.

It was now or never. She had to say the words aloud whether or not he accepted them or whether he rejected her. "I'm not playing, Logan."

His cat eyes narrowed, gleaming with a searing intent that almost scared her. She was so willing to follow her heart in this, but did it mean that she was being a fool by pushing Logan's restraint to the limit?

"There is one thing your mother should have taught you about shifters, angel," he said, his voice dark and gravelly. "We don't possess human traits of restraint. When a shifter wants something or someone—he takes her." He glared hard at her. "And he doesn't look back, afterwards."

Her heart sang. He did want her! And even though she heard his warning loud and clear, she couldn't help but be happy that he had admitted his desire.

A brief moment of clarity made her accept the fact that his attraction could very well be because of her mating cycle. He'd said other shifters wouldn't be able to resist her during this time. With him being the exception, of course.

Tara took a deep fortifying breath and released it slowly. She wasn't going to turn back now. She wanted this, wanted him, with every fiber in her being. She would face what was to come, and accept the consequences for her action.

"If you want me to get dressed, Logan," she said softly, "Then you'll have to give me back my panties."

A startled look of surprise crossed his face for one brief moment. But then, it was replaced with something dark and intense, something that warned her that she should be tread carefully with tempting the beast inside him. He looked down at the panties in his hand. He slowly raised them to his face.

Tara's knees buckled and she nearly fell when he pressed the silky material to his nose and breathed in a deep inhale. She'd never been faced with such eroticism before and it hit her like a blow to the stomach, leaving her breathless and shocked. And ... on fire.

Logan's nostrils flared as he took in several deep breaths, and he closed his eyes with a hungry groan. The sound echoed through the room and hit Tara like a physical touch, leaving her shivering in the wake.

Her entire body was on fire, every sense heightened to painful awareness of the need that radiated off Logan then. For one second her mind forced doubts to surface. If he was this intense ... and hadn't even touched her yet, could she handle any more?

"Logan?" His name escaped her parted lips on a whispered plea. She needed him to do something, anything, to keep her from giving in to the doubts and fear. But if he rejected her, she was sure she would die.

He looked at her, his breathing harsh now. "You're killing me, angel," he grated out and threw the panties to the floor. "I can't fight this need. It has been burning inside me from the first moment we met. You belong to another man, and yet all I can think of is taking you and making you mine." He ran a shaky hand over his face. "But you can't be mine. Even if we take tonight ... I will still hand you over to Damian tomorrow. It has to be that way, Tara."

Despite knowing what he said was true, it still hurt. Her heart and soul realized that she was falling in love with Logan. But he didn't feel the same way. He could admit his desire for her—and most likely that was because she was a beacon right now to any shifter—but he wasn't willing to give in to any other feelings or explanations.

Okay, I have to accept that. If I want this night, then I have to accept that it means nothing more to him than a one-night stand induced by pheromones.

She made up her mind. And her heart.

"Give me tonight, Logan," she pleaded softly. "And I won't fight you tomorrow. I'll go to Damian."

His stare was so intense and his silence too long. She realized she was holding her breath and released it on a defeated sigh.

"Come here."

Tara gasped. Before she could change her mind she took a hesitant step forward then stopped. Her heart was beating so hard and fast that she was sure he could hear it across the room.

Logan growled under his breath. "If I come to you, angel, then I'll never know that you really wanted this. You have to come to me."

They were the easiest … and the hardest steps she'd ever taken in her life. She stopped in front of him and raised her gaze to his. She reached up and touched his cheek with a soft caress. "Make tonight last for as long as possible," she whispered. "Please, Logan."

He grasped her hand and brought it to his lips to press a hot kiss into her palm. "I intend to, Tara." The words sounded torn from the depths of his soul, touching her like nothing else had. "I just pray I have the strength to let you go when the morning comes."

He released her hand and gathered her into his arms. Tara put her arms around his neck when he lifted her up and carried her to the bed. She suddenly felt nervous and hid her face against his throat. The growl that rumbled from him vibrated against her cheek.

Logan placed her in the center of the bed and then stepped back. He stood staring down at her for long, tense moments. "Just for tonight," he murmured. Tara wanted to ask him what he meant, but was completely mesmerized as he slowly began taking off his shirt. He dropped it to the floor. He sat down in the chair beside the bed and pulled off his boots. Never releasing her from his searing gaze, he stood up and unfastened his jeans.

Tara's breath caught and she forgot to breathe when he slowly shoved the jeans down his thighs and legs and pulled them off.

He wasn't wearing underwear.

He stood proud, looking down at her, and she couldn't tear

her gaze away from his strong, virile body. His body was a tanned masterpiece from head to toes. A dark sprinkling of brandy-brown hair across his chest narrowed down to his flat stomach and then to his groin.

His erection stood at attention, and Tara couldn't tear her gaze away from it. He was huge. A tiny moment of panic hit. She couldn't remember Mark being that large. In fact, his had been small and not so ... pulsing. She swallowed a groan. Logan was so incredibly—male.

"This is your fault," he muttered with a smile that seemed strained. "I've been in this state since day one around you."

"I'm sorry." But she wasn't! She smiled back. "But you were in cat form those first hours."

"Yeah, but I had very human male thoughts the entire time. Especially when you stepped out of that shower. I thought I was going to change right then and expose myself." He grinned again. "In more ways than one."

She giggled. "Can you imagine what would have happened if you had changed just as Mara came in?"

"No. But I could easily imagine what would have happened if I would have changed while we were alone."

Tara's breath caught at the silky threat. She tried to sound nonchalant as she countered, "If you had changed, I'd have run. As fast and as far as I could."

Logan's hot gaze seared her. "And I would have caught you."

"What if I had managed to get away and you never found me again?" she asked. "What would you have done then?"

Logan braced a knee on the bed and leaned forward. "I had your scent, angel. I could find you anywhere in the entire world."

She lowered her eyes. "I suppose you're right. I've heard that shifters are the best hunters in the world." She had been a mission to him, prey that he was determined to capture no matter the cost or time.

"We are," he agreed. He came onto the bed and stretched out beside her. "But that wasn't the reason I could have found you, Tara."

He reached out and touched her cheek, caressed over it and then down to her parted lips. His look darkened. "I have your scent in my memory. My body. I always will."

What was he saying? Dared she hope? "Shifters don't forget the scent of their prey?"

Logan pressed a finger against her bottom lip. A muscle ticked in his jaw. "We don't forget the scent of the one we claim. We can't forget."

She was more confused now than before. "But you haven't claimed me, Logan."

He grinned slowly, the smile so sexy and so possessive that she thought her heart would burst with the chaotic emotions racing through her.

"They're only words, Tara. Words that mean nothing right now. It's time to stop thinking. I've always been a firm believer that action is a lot better than just words."

Tara's heart sang. She didn't want to analyze what he truly meant—right now was the only thing important. She smiled and opened her mouth to lightly nip his finger pressed there.

"Are you going to kiss me anytime soon? That would be a wonderful action ..."

Logan chuckled, the sound husky and sexy. "Yeah. I'm going to kiss you. And ... do a lot more action before this night is through."

Tara's last coherent thought was entirely wishful. *Goddess, please make this night last forever.*

Chapter Fourteen

Logan's hand moved away from her mouth and slowly caressed across her cheek and down to her throat. His gaze followed the path of his hand. His touch was gentle despite the heat radiating off him in waves.

"Your skin is so soft," he whispered. "I've wanted to touch you ever since I first saw you naked from the shower. I knew you would feel like silk."

His hand continued a slow descent down her throat and across her collarbone and shoulder. He stopped at the edge of the bath towel above her breasts. He lifted his gaze back to hers. "I want to touch all of you."

She couldn't utter a sound as he dipped his fingers below the towel's edge and slowly pulled the material away. She had twisted it closed in front, so with a slight tug the towel parted and fell away from her body. She held her breath.

Logan hissed in a deep breath. He let it out on a rough groan. "You're so damn beautiful," he choked out hoarsely. His searing, hungry gaze traveled from her face to her throat, to her breasts, lingered there, then moved slowly down her stomach.

He closed his eyes tight for a moment, and made the effort to slow his breathing. She watched the struggle for control flash over his features. Her heart raced and she tried to slow her own breathing.

Logan opened his eyes and stared down at her. Holding her gaze with his, he slowly reached out and palmed her left breast in his hand. Tara lost her breath completely. His large hand cupped her breast and squeezed lightly, and then he ran his thumb over her extended nipple, back and forth. "Pebbled berries," he murmured hungrily. Tara closed her eyes and reminded herself to breathe as

Logan lowered his head.

His hot lips pressed a kiss across the top of her breast, and lingered there for a moment. That moment was excruciating. Tara heard her own choked voice beg, "Please," and then felt his smile against her skin as his lips pressed another kiss in the same spot.

Logan's lips moved down and before she could utter a gasp he closed his mouth around her nipple and sucked deep.

Tara moaned and arched up into the heat. He sucked harder, his hand holding her breast and squeezing with every draw of his mouth. His hot, rough tongue rasped over the nipple as he sucked and Tara was awash in drowning waves of pleasure.

Suddenly Logan released her breast and moved to give her right one a brief kiss. He raised his head and stared down into her eyes. His hand moved from her breast to slowly caress down her stomach. Tara was acutely aware of every inch he touched. She held her own hands clenched at her side. Now she reached up and touched his mouth, marveling at the heat still radiating there. Logan opened his mouth and bit down lightly on her fingers. He groaned. She raised questioning brows.

"I have to keep reminding myself —you're a human," he muttered in answer.

"What does that have to do with … now?"

"A shifters mating is different, angel. I can't take you the way I want to, need to. I have to stay in control, but I'm not sure I'll be able to."

He wasn't going to stop now was he? No! Tara wasn't going to let him go. He had promised her tonight and she wasn't going to let him walk away. She needed him. More than she'd ever needed anyone in her entire life.

"I'm yours, Logan," she whispered, her very heart and soul in those words. "Just for tonight, there's nothing to keep us apart. Don't think about anything else. Please. Just … love me."

Logan groaned and closed his eyes. "Loving you is going to be the easy part, angel," he said, the choked-out words barely audible. "Letting you go is going to kill me."

What was he saying? Tara's heart sang. Were his feelings for her deeper than just desire? She wanted to believe that. Desperately.

Tara tangled both her hands in his hair and ran them through the long, thick length to his shoulders. She rested her hands lightly on his shoulders. She watched his mental struggle as his jaw clenched and his eyes turned darker. They shone with a deep fire that seemed to burn her as he stared down into her face. There was a look of primal possessiveness shining in the blue depths, a look of stark need that made her breath catch in her throat.

Tara pushed away any last, lingering thoughts of doubt. For the rest of her life she would remember the look in Logan's eyes in that precise moment she knew he had decided there was no turning back.

"Love me," she whispered softly. "Take me the way you would if I was a shifter, too."

Logan's harsh growl rumbled against her mouth as he took her lips in a deep, possessive kiss. Tara wrapped her arms around his neck. He came over her then, his hard body moving to cover her completely.

Naked flesh against naked flesh. The feeling was incredible. Tara arched up into him and kissed him back. His tongue swept her mouth, its hot, raspy texture more erotic than she'd ever dreamed any thing could be. The thought of his tongue touching her on other parts of her body sent a shiver of anticipation through her that settled deep in the pit of her stomach.

Logan kissed her like a man starved, and their mouths clung to the others, until they were both too breathless and had to break apart to catch their breaths.

Then Logan uttered those words she'd heard earlier, "Just for tonight."

Tara wanted to scream in protest, *No! Not just for tonight. Please let it be forever!* But the protest was locked in her throat when Logan lowered his head and licked a long searing path down her stomach from her breasts. His raspy tongue was hot, rough, and he licked every inch of her stomach. Tara squirmed and arched up to meet the erotic torture.

Logan grasped her hips with his hands as he suddenly lifted his head and looked back at her. There was wildness in his eyes, a fierce need that scorched her. She met his gaze with all the love she felt inside. She didn't care if he saw it for what it was.

Logan's hold on her hips tightened. She felt the intended warning and held her breath. With one last, deep look in her eyes, he slowly lowered his head. Tara bit down on her bottom lip to keep from crying out as he scooted lower and she suddenly felt his hot lips, then his tongue, just below her navel.

With excruciating slowness, Logan licked her skin with long raspy swipes, and moved inch by inch lower to his destination. Her entire body stiffened with heightened anticipation as he stopped at the waxed area of her feminine mound.

Tara felt his body suddenly stiffen. Before she could wonder why, he exhaled sharply and she felt a long swipe of his tongue over her. She cried out, the sharp streak of pleasure arcing through her. Logan placed a heavy arm across her stomach and held her down. "I want to taste you."

It was all the warning she had. His hard tongue delved deep into her burning center. She lost her breath completely. Her vision swam. Her entire body shook with a need she didn't even recognize.

Logan's tongue dived in and out, stabbing into her with a rough hunger that shook her to the depths of her being. Her head writhed on the pillow and her body writhed beneath the arm he was holding her down with.

Then, Logan's tongue touched the very center of her. A ragged, hungry groan escaped him and he circled her with another hard swipe. He opened his mouth wide and sucked. Hard. Hungrily.

Tara screamed. She dug her hands into his hair and pulled. Swirls of kaleidoscopic colors swam in her vision. Her body shook with unfamiliar ecstasy that crashed over her in waves. Logan sucked greedily, and the waves battered her relentlessly.

The erotic assault was almost too much. She cried out, begging for something she wasn't sure of, "Logan, please!"

He didn't let up. The sensual fire built inside her, spread straight to her womb. Another forceful wave, stronger than before, built in intensity, rose to consume her. She wanted to beg him to stop. She prayed he never would.

The wave hit her. Hard. Breath-stealing. She screamed as the orgasm streaked through her. Spasms of indescribable pleasure rolled over every inch of her. Then, she went limp, breathless and dizzy, as the aftershocks of the orgasm slowly faded away into small, tingling tremors.

Logan slowly lifted his head and their gazes locked—his burning with a dark, intense, hunger that showed no softening.

"That was the sweetest thing I've ever tasted," he said roughly, his voice harsh with relentless need.

She couldn't have said anything even if she wanted to. He didn't give her the chance anyway. He moved to cover her body again with his. His hands grasped her thighs and opened her just enough for him to settle his hard, pulsing erection directly between the aching spot of her center. Every inch of him that touched her was hard, hot, and she wanted to arch again into all that primal maleness. She wanted something, desperately, that she couldn't put a name to. It was a deep and painful aching need that spread through her and threatened to consume her.

Logan caressed down her leg and then up again. When he reached her knee he lifted her leg and positioned it against his hip. The position pushed him closer against her mound and she shivered uncontrollably with the searing need that hit her then.

Logan's body stiffened. "Are you afraid of me, Tara?"

She heard the vulnerable sound in his words and shook her head. "You make me feel things I never dreamed of."

"Are you sure of this? Can you take all I want to do to you? Are you willing to sacrifice everything for just tonight?"

She didn't even have to think about it. Her answer was vehemently heartfelt. "Yes."

Logan lowered his head and kissed her. The touch of his lips was gentle, surprising her. And then he purred.

That sound was more erotic than any she had ever heard as it vibrated against her mouth. It called to something wild inside her that she didn't realize existed. Something hidden deep and just waiting for the time when that part of her soul would be claimed by something as wild.

Logan kissed his way across her cheek and then to her ear; his purring echoed there with an unspoken promise. His hot lips caressed down her throat to her shoulder.

A growl, primal and rough, rumbled from his chest into hers. He suddenly sank his teeth into the tender skin of her shoulder, marking her as his.

A small scream broke from Tara, shocking her with the stark need that burned from the spot on her neck all the way to her very soul. She grasped Logan's head and held him there, reveling in the sharp grip of his teeth, his rough heavy breathing against her skin.

She heard her own voice, crying out, encouraging him, "Yes!"

over and over.

Logan suddenly reared his head. He stared down at her, his breathing harsh, rough, his eyes searing fire. Tara felt the tension in his body as he grasped her hands and brought them up to rest on her pillow beside her head. He settled deeper into the vee of her body.

He purred. Once. Rough. The sound a triumphant declaration.

With one single, hard thrust, he entered her.

Tara screamed out, the ecstasy too much to bear. The pleasure pain was overwhelming. He was huge, scorching hot, pulsing hard. Never in her wildest dreams had she ever thought it would feel this incredible.

Logan settled heavier against her, his body tense and hard as he held still for long moments and waited for her body to accommodate his invasion. Tara forced herself to breathe deep. The movement pushed her breasts up against his chest and he groaned loudly.

She whispered his name, a plea she wasn't sure of, "Logan."

"Yes!" Logan hissed through clenched teeth. He released her hands and grasped her hips with a painfully tight grip.

Tara would later wonder if she'd heard correctly. He lowered his head and whispered one word against her lips as he started to move deep within her, "Mine."

His thrusts were incredibly slow, almost controlled, yet completely possessive. He pushed deep into her, touching her womb, and then withdrew. Over and over again Logan thrust into her and kept his mouth hard over hers. Their breaths mingled, and their hearts beat in perfect rhythm. Tara tried to arch up to meet his every thrust, but his grip on her hips held her still.

She wanted. Needed something. Frustration mounted with her desire. Logan was holding back, she knew it. Tara jerked her head aside, breaking the kiss, and choked out a desperate plea, "Please, Logan. Love me. Don't hold back."

"Tara," he gasped out her name on a harsh breath. "You don't realize what you're asking. Hold still, angel. Let me love you this way."

"No," she struggled slightly and his thrusts stopped. "I want it all. Let me have tonight and everything it can be."

Logan's grip on her hips tightened so painfully that she gasped aloud. He suddenly rose above her, his features harsh and dark. His passionate expression took her breath away.

"Sweet Tara. First for you," he muttered. "And then … for me."

Tara didn't understand for a moment. Then she felt his finger slip deep inside her and his thrusts suddenly became faster. Before she could rise up to meet his thrusts, his finger touched her and circled. And she exploded.

Stars burst in brilliant colors behind her closed lids. Waves of drowning ecstasy rushed over her, building with such painful intensity she was sure she wouldn't survive it. Logan tightened his hold and his thrusts increased to match the devouring wave as the orgasm hit her.

She cried out his name as the orgasm stole her breath and every coherent thought.

Logan stilled, his body heavy on her as the slowly receding waves rippled through her.

Tara's body relaxed, a sweet euphoria settling over her. Her mind cleared and she was instantly aware of Logan laying so stiffly over her. She ran her hands down his sleek back. "Logan?"

He stared down into her eyes. His lips formed into a thin slash as though he was holding back words he didn't want to say. Tara caressed over his lips with a soft touch. "What?"

His voice was low, deep, when he finally answered, "If I hurt you —or scare you, tell me to stop. I swear I will. I won't do anything that you don't want me to. Just tell me to stop."

Her heart melted. Despite his obvious need, he was giving her the choice to say no before he did anything else. Her heart stuttered then. There was … more?

She met his hungry gaze with all the trust she possessed. "I trust you, Logan. For tonight, I'm yours. In every way."

Logan slowly withdrew from her body. She felt immediately bereft. He sat up. He laid a hot hand over her mound, and caressed it with a lingering touch. "Roll over, angel."

Heart racing, desire beginning to build again, Tara didn't hesitate. She rolled over to lie on her stomach. She turned her head sideways on the pillow and looked back at him. His hot gaze was on her buttocks. He reached out a hand and caressed the twin globes.

"Every inch of you turns me on," he muttered. "I want to mark you, everywhere. I want to put love bites on every sweet, silky inch of you, and then lick the spots over and over."

The vivid mental picture of him doing just that was enough to start her body shivering in sweet anticipation. But Logan mistook the shivering for something else.

"Don't worry, angel. I won't." His expression darkened. "The last thing you need is to have a cat's mark all over you when—Damian claims you."

Tara gasped at the harsh words. "Stop, Logan. Don't bring Damian into this. I can't bear the thought …"

Logan uttered a stark expletive under his breath. He came down over her, blanketing her body with his, grabbing her hands and pulling them away from the pillow. He entwined their hands, moving them to above her head, and buried his face against the back of her neck.

"Then, don't think. Just feel. Feel. Just. Me."

Logan shoved her legs apart with his knee and settled between them, pushing against the opening of her there. Tara tensed, yet the feeling of him there wasn't unpleasant. It was a tingling feeling of untamed eroticism she'd never experienced before.

He released one of her hands and grasped a handful of her hair to shove it aside and bare her shoulder. His rough purr was the only warning. His teeth latched onto the same spot he'd bit earlier.

Tara cried out with the pleasure-pain and the sound ended on a choked gasp as Logan suddenly surged forward and buried his shaft deep inside her.

Every muscle in her body tightened in surprising acceptance of the invasion. She pushed back against him, mindless with the need for something she couldn't put a name to.

It was the only encouragement Logan needed. He thrust hard. Deep. Their world turned into a mindless, all-feeling bubble of never ending fervor and soul-consuming passion as Logan claimed her body, over and over.

Their cries mingled. Their bodies clung to each other. The world narrowed down to just them. His body claiming hers in the most primal way a man could, and hers taking everything he had to give, accepting the wildness with a heart that cried for even more.

Their world exploded. Logan's final thrust touched her all the way to her soul. He shouted her name, the sound an odd, mixed cry of defeat and victory.

As their bodies violently shook in the aftermath, Tara heard his

hoarse whisper,
  "Mine. Just for tonight."

Chapter Fifteen

The cool air in the room settled over their still bodies and soothed their harsh breathing into soft breaths that mingled as Logan turned Tara over and pulled her into his arms.

They lay like that for a long time. Tara rested her head against his chest and listened to the hard beating of his heart. Hers beat just as hard. Her body ached in places she hadn't known a man would ever touch like that, before tonight. The bite on her shoulder was still stinging a little and it was a stark reminder that Logan had claimed her as a shifter would during a mating. She wondered if the mark was permanent.

She wanted it to be.

Logan stirred. He lightly ran his hands over her back in a gentle caress. He purred softly, the sound content—a male shifter satisfied with the all-consuming sexual claiming of a mate.

"I love that sound," Tara whispered against his chest.

"Cat shifters purr for different reasons," he commented, sounding as though his thoughts were far away. "It's part of our nature to express our feelings that way."

"There's so much I don't know." She knew that was admitting her vulnerabilities but she couldn't stop the words.

Logan didn't respond. Tara lifted her head and searched his face. His expression was dark again, his narrow cat eyes shining with an odd gleam of something she couldn't comprehend. "What are you thinking?"

•

Could he tell her? Say the stark words aloud and shock that contented look right off her beautiful face?

This night isn't over. I haven't even begun to love you like I want to, like I need to.

That one coupling hadn't been enough. There was still so many ways he wanted to claim her, brand her as his own. His body still pulsed with the hungry need; it felt like it was consuming him.

But she's not yours, you fool. Damn, when had this situation got out of control? When had he allowed his feelings for this woman to override his conscience and his honor to keep a promise?

"You're thinking about Damian."

He sighed. "Yeah."

"I don't feel guilty, Logan. I wanted this with all my heart. I know I can't run from my destiny anymore. I will go to Damian, but even though he claims me as his wife and Queen, I won't give him my soul." She rose up, propping herself on his chest. She touched his cheek, caressed over his hard lips. "I will keep this night in my heart forever. No matter what happens now. I won't let your guilt make me regret any moment."

"Even when it means you go to Damian with my mark on you?"

She smiled at the possessive growl in his tone. "Then, it's permanent?"

"Damn it, Tara. Don't act so happy about that. If I'd had an ounce of sense left in me, I wouldn't have marked you. Damian is a formable shifter. He isn't going to be happy about that mark, especially when he'll know I did it." He wasn't afraid of Damian's anger; he could kill the damn shifter in an instant. But the thought of the wolf shifter turning his wrath on Tara made him sick to his stomach. He wouldn't be there to protect her …

"Why should it matter?" She frowned at him. "As long as I mate with Damian and my Goddess powers are shared with him, then he shouldn't care what happened before." She suddenly paled. She leaned back a little from him. "Logan," she hesitated then continued, "Why didn't that happen between us?"

Logan knew what she was talking about. And he knew the answer. He just wasn't sure how he felt about it. The implications were just as confusing as his feelings were right then.

"You aren't in the mating cycle any more, Tara."

She gasped. "What? How can you know that?"

He grinned, all male in the knowledge. "When I sniffed your panties I could tell the cycle had passed. Then, when I tasted your sweet juices I was positive."

Tara blushed prettily. He grinned again. After all they had just shared she was still able to blush at his stark words.

"I don't understand how or why," he confessed as the thought hit him, "but your cycle was only a twenty-four hour time. You should have been in a forty-eight hour cycle like the wolf shifter females. Instead, your body reacted the way a cat shifter female would. I would have thought that the Goddess would have your body prepared for a wolf shifter alliance in every aspect."

Tara's intent gaze was flying over his face. She opened her mouth to say something, closed it, then opened it again. Finally she blurted out in a breathless tone, "I wasn't in my mating cycle when we made love?"

"No."

He was leery of the question, unsure of what was coming. He wanted to make love to her again. Forget about Damian. Forget about mating cycles. Forget about tomorrow.

"Then my cycle didn't influence your response to me?"

Damn. He hadn't meant for her to realize that. "No."

"Why did you make love to me, Logan? Was it only because I asked you to?"

Logan never knew what he might have answered. A loud crash downstairs startled them both. He shoved Tara to his side and jumped from the bed. He willed on clothes and was halfway down the stairs before Tara could finish calling out his name.

He should have been more alert. He knew there were other shifters in the area. How the hell they'd tracked Tara here, considering she wasn't in her mating cycle now, was something he didn't want to dwell on. That would mean he hadn't been careful, he hadn't protected her like he should have.

He came down the stairs in a preternatural flash of movement, ready to attack. The two wolf shifters met him in mid air and the three clashed with a loud collision. Logan fought with a rage that burned deep. He landed several damaging blows to his opponents before they managed to get the upper hand on him and take him to the floor. Three more shifters joined in and Logan found himself under a barrage of fists and claws that struck hard and fast. Within moments he knew he was losing this fight. The thought of Tara burned through him. He made a last effort to break away.

A heavy blow to his head was Logan's last coherent realization.

Everything went black.

•

Tara was barely finished dressing when the shifters came up the stairs to the loft bedroom. She backed away as the men approached her. Her heart raced and she felt sick to her stomach. Logan was no where in sight. She refused to allow herself to think about what that meant.

"Who are you and what do you want?" She tried to sound brave but heard the quiver in her voice. *Logan, help!*

One of the men, the tallest, chuckled. "I don't think you're that naïve, little goddess. The real question here is whether or not you are going to fight us, or come willingly?"

Tara stood her ground. "I'm not going anywhere with you. Where's Logan? What did you do to him?"

"Beat him to a bloody mess," another man answered smugly. "Wanna take a look?"

Tara's stomach clenched and she was afraid she'd be sick. Tears stung her eyes but she refused to cry in front of these jerks. She stared at them—five well-muscled men she had no chance of escaping from. If she tried to fight, chances were that she'd only end up worse off. If she went willingly, maybe they would leave Logan behind and he would have the chance to come after her. She didn't know how bad he was hurt, but she consoled herself with the reminder that he'd once said shifters healed quickly.

"Where are you taking me? To Damian?" If that was the destination, then she didn't have much to fear.

One of the men shook his head and spit out a foul word. "You don't belong with that weakling shifter. There is another more worthy of your Goddess powers. Our Prince should be the chosen one."

Who was he talking about? She thought Damian was the only Prince of the wolf shifters in the United States. She looked at the men closely. There was something different about them. They were darker skinned than most Americans, and now that she noticed it their speech was tainted with an accent.

"Who?" It didn't matter. If she was being kidnapped and taken from Damian, things were worse than she'd thought.

"Our Prince reigns over the Greek Isles. He is mightier than Damian, and plans to rule the entire world's clans. You are destined for him, and no other."

Not if he was the last man on earth! Tara grimaced. The thought was brave but inconsequential. Her life depended now on going with them and hoping for escape later. She raised her chin and marched past the men and down the stairs.

At the bottom of the stairs she screamed and fell forward to her knees beside Logan's unconscious form. He was a beat up, bloodied mess and she wasn't even sure he was still alive. "Oh, Goddess! Logan!"

The tears she'd tried to hold back fell now and she brokenly called out his name over and over. *Please, don't be dead. Logan, breathe, please!* But he never moved, never responded in the slightest way. Pain clutched at her heart and Tara thought she would die from its intensity.

One of the shifters reached down and pulled her roughly to her feet. With a shove, he pushed her out the cabin door. Tara turned to take one last look at Logan. His bloodied, unconscious form was imbedded in her mind and she stumbled away with the painful fear that she'd never see him again.

They walked for over an hour, deep into the forest and then out to the other side. Tara was heartsick and exhausted, and kept stumbling. Her captors weren't happy with her and made no pretense of showing they were. She was pushed, cursed at, and roughly handled all the way to their destination.

By the time they reached the caves on the other side of the lake, Tara was fed up. She turned on them, and looked each one over from head to toes, her gaze thorough. "Don't think I'll conveniently forget any of you or your courtesy after I become your Queen." She let the threat hang in the air. They stared at her in obvious surprise at her outburst. She raised her head and marched forward. *There! Let them worry about that!*

She studied the caves that were dotted along the hillside by the lake. They all had small openings, and she couldn't count how many of them there were. Was this where Senya and Eric lived? Hope surged. Would they help her?

The hope didn't last. When she was ushered into the largest dark cave, she found herself in the midst of a cavern peopled with shifters. Who were obviously just as much prisoners as she was now.

Chapter Sixteen

Damian watched as his bodyguard slammed Colin to the ground. His brother was back on his feet in an instant and charging into the guard with a ferocious growl.

"Your response is fast," he stated. "But you shouldn't have given Zean a chance to knock you down in the first place."

Colin threw his brother a dirty look and slammed hard into Zean. The guard went down and Colin growled triumphantly as he pinned him to the ground.

Since his recovery from the attack, Colin had been in training again. Damian wasn't taking any chances. Colin had been only second best to him as a fighter, but the damage done to his body had slowed him some and neither brother was happy with that.

Neither brother thought about it, but it was an undeniable fact that should something happen to Damian then Colin would take his place as Prince. They were the only two left of the Royal line in the United States. It was an unspoken hope that Damian's marriage to Tara would produce male offspring so the Sinclair line would continue. Colin was as yet unmated, but should something happen to Damian he would step in as Prince and rule by Tara's side. It was a plan his brother wasn't happy about, but Damian knew he would carry it out if the time came.

Damian stretched painful, aching muscles. *The time may come sooner than we expect.* The strange illness affecting him was making each day harder to get through.

Colin approached his brother. "You're tired already this morning," he said with quiet concern. "Why don't you visit the healer again? I'll lead the pack later and hunt for you while you rest."

"I can't show weakness, Colin. Our enemies are just waiting for a chance to strike."

"Let them. I'll be ready this time. Bastards! They had to have help from a human to take me down the first time. They won't get that chance again."

Colin's confidence gave Damian a spark of hope. It also reminded him of what he wanted to talk to him about. "Logan should be arriving today or tomorrow at the latest. I want extra guards posted to watch over Tara. Her human frailty will be a beacon to our enemies."

"Doesn't she have Goddess powers to protect herself with?"

"Not yet. That was part of the Prophecy. She will only come into her powers once she is united—physically—with her destined mate. Until we are married, she is vulnerable."

"I'll hand-pick her guards and make sure they're the best we have," Colin promised.

Damian thanked him and left to find Emily. There were things he had to say to her before Tara arrived today. Things he had left unsaid for too long.

•

Two lone wolf shifters moved stealthily from their hiding place as they watched Damian and Colin walk away.

"We have to make sure Colin chooses both of us for that guard team," one said. "We haven't heard from the others, so there's no way to know if they have found the Goddess mate yet. If they fail in their plan to capture her before the Cat brings her here, then we have to be in place to follow through."

"Considering that we both share the Sinclair blood as cousins to the Princes, Colin is sure to choose us. I don't see any problems."

"Let's make sure everything is in place. If we fail in this, then everything we've been promised is forfeit."

They slinked away. Neither one noticed the female wolf standing five yards away. They had spoken in soft wolf tones and she hadn't heard every word. But, she heard enough to know that they were up to no good. She hurried away to find Damian.

•

Tara choked back her surprise and shock as she surveyed the cave's interior filled with prisoners. And she knew that's what they were; they sat huddled together against the cave's wall and behind a strange barrier that looked like a three-feet-high wall of bricks. She frowned. How the heck did such a small wall keep them inside?

Her gaze flew over the faces of the prisoners until she found the two she was looking for. Senya sat cuddled in Erik's arms. He was a handsome shifter, dark haired and well muscled. Tara glanced at his left arm and saw that his hand was still bandaged from his run in with the trap. *That doesn't make sense*, she thought, Logan said *shifters heal quickly. And he shouldn't have been able to change back to man while he was still wounded.*

She didn't have time to dwell on it. The tall shifter who had been bullying her every step of the way now shoved her from behind.

"Heads up, Goddess," he said. "One of us is going to have to lift you over the barrier. I don't want you fighting him when he touches you."

Before she could protest, one of the shifters strode forward and grabbed her. He lifted her in his arms and had her over the barrier in mere moments. One the other side of the wall Tara's feet landed in a thin stream of water that ran along the entire length of the wall. The stream was only a few inches deep, but at least a foot wide, and was an odd silver color. When she stepped out of it, a coating of silver like that of filmy glue stuck to her shoes. She shook it off and then watched in surprised fascination as the residue flowed, straight back into the stream as if magnetized to do so.

She turned to find Senya and Erik by her side, their faces showing concern. "What's happening?" she asked, "Why are you prisoners?"

Erik frowned darkly and growled under his breath. "We were caught, completely off guard, when the Greek Pack came into our area. Our males were hunting miles away and the women were at the lake gathering herbs. The children were in the caves, safe, but the few sentry guards were unprepared for the whole pack to attack. They took our children and then the women. We had no choice but to surrender."

"Why did they do this? Is it normal for an outside pack to overrun another?" Tara wished she had taken the time to learn more about the shifters and their world. But she'd been so determined to avoid that world at all cost. That was stupid. A little more knowledge right now might be a big help.

Her mind turned to Logan. Was he still unconscious? Or ... worse? Would he heal quickly and come after her? She looked at Erik's hand. "What happened? Shouldn't you be healed now?"

Erik nodded. "I was. But after I'd changed back to man, one of the shifters decided to slice the wound open again." His expression was dangerously angry. "They've injured us all, in one way or another, to keep us from changing back to our wolf forms."

Tara felt sick. "Even the children?"

Senya nodded, tears in her eyes. "Thank the Goddess that all it takes to keep us from changing is a little wound. The children were all sliced in their hands, just a small wound but enough to be effective. The rest of us have been wounded in other spots, the women mostly in their legs."

Tara cringed. This was a nightmare. It was bad enough that a species would willingly harm another of their own kind, but to deliberately hurt children was just too much for her to think about. She glanced back over her shoulder. "What about this wall? It's so low, surely you could jump it easily even in human form."

"No," Erik rumbled angrily. "The stream is filled with pure silver. Just being inches near it can kill us, or disable us to a severe extreme. If it got on our skin it would kill us almost immediately."

"Goddess," Tara murmured. What were they going to do? "Why have they taken you prisoner? And why did they bring me here?"

Senya answered. "Our pack supports Prince Damian's claim to be the Ruler and mate with the Goddess Child of Prophecy. You. We were planning to move to Riverside Park and merge with his immediate pack in order to unify the force of supporters. Our men are some of the best fighters and Damian will need an army to back him. Unfortunately, our men are not trained to fight with the weapons this Greek Pack has. They were able to disable us with the pure silver—even killing a few of the men as examples—and force our surrender."

"The only reason I can think of for bringing you here is because this is where they managed to capture you and it was best to keep you here until the others arrived," Erik said.

"Others? There are more bad shifters coming?" Tara bit back a groan of dismay. "Just great." Could this situation get any worse? Even if Logan managed to survive that attack and then track her down, what chance did he stand against so many powerful wolf shifters? "We have to do something. We can't just be meek victims." Tara rubbed at her forehead, an ache pounding behind her temples.

The instant she touched her brows a strange tingle shivered

from the palms of her hand, into her fingers, and straight into her forehead. The ache disappeared immediately. She shook her head, surprised. Maybe she had just imagined the ache? She stared down at her still-tingling fingers. What was going on?

"Your hands," Senya gasped. "They have a glowing aura!"

Tara stared hard but couldn't see it. "Are you sure? Why can't I see it?"

"It's faint, but a shifter can see auras like that."

"Why is my hand shining?" *And why am I suddenly feeling very different? As though there is an energy force building inside me?* Was she coming into some of her Goddess powers? But that couldn't be possible. That was only to happen after she mated with Damian. Maybe the Goddess Azina was sending her aid now, so that she could help the shifters? It was the only explanation she could think of. Nothing else made sense.

Tara met Erik's intent gaze. She wanted to test her theory. "Give me your hand."

He didn't question her, just held out his bandaged hand. Tara took it between both hers and held it lightly. Instantly the tingling in her palms and then her fingers increased. A slight wave of heat radiated from her hands to Erik's injured one. Just for added measure she focused on visualizing his wound healed.

Tara released Erik's hand and asked him to take the bandage off. When he did, the wound was completely healed. Not even a scar remained. They gasped in unison.

Tara didn't know what to think about this new talent. She'd always been able to perform simple magicks—it was part of her heritage—but never something this dramatic. Maybe she'd had the healing power all along and just never had the legitimate reason for using it?

"How did you do that?" Senya examined Erik's hand, her dark eyes wide.

Erik quickly hushed his mate. "We don't want the guards to hear."

They looked at the front of the cave where four guards stood sentry. Luck was on their side that once they had been placed securely behind the wall and silver stream they were no longer considered a threat to the Greek Pack, so the guards paid them no attention.

"I'm not sure what's going on," Tara said, "But let's see if I can heal the others too. Then we can figure out a way to get you all out of here before those bullies come back."

Erik quietly introduced her to the pack. Just like Senya's first reaction, they stared at Tara in awe and admiration. One by one she proceeded to heal each shifter of their wounds. It was a slow process because they didn't want to draw any attention to her moving among them, and by the time she was finished with the last shifter she was exhausted.

She didn't think she had ever felt this drained in all her life. She slumped to the ground and let out a tired sigh. Her vision was blurry, her limbs were lead weight, and her head was pounding all over again.

Senya brought her a cup of fresh water. "Will you be all right, dear Tara?"

Tara nodded. "I just need to rest for a bit." She looked at the children shifters. Their young faces were filled with shining hope and their gazes were locked on her in complete worship. She smiled encouragingly at them. "Make sure the children stay quiet. We don't want the guards to know they are no longer injured. Don't let any of them change."

Senya hurried away to do as she bid. Erik sat down beside Tara. "I noticed that the silver didn't harm you. That may give us an advantage they didn't anticipate."

"What can we do?" She was so exhausted she wasn't sure she'd be able to move for awhile even if her life depended on it.

"You can step over the stream and the wall. We'll wait until tonight when the guards are eating. At the back of this cave is an opening that leads to the outside and straight into the woods. You can escape." He studied Tara's face for a long moment. "I don't know where your Cat protector is, but it won't be safe for you to return to the cabin to look for him there. If he survived the attack, then chances are he will be searching for you, but he'll realize he will need help in fighting this Pack. He may search for other Cat shifters and then come back. By then, you can be far away. Go back to your own people for protection. Let them get you safely to Damian after this battle is finished."

Escape? Return home? The possibilities flew through her chaotic thoughts. If she escaped, would she take the chance to run even farther? To get away from here, from Damian, and ... from Logan?

No. She couldn't do it. No matter what was to come, she knew she couldn't run away again. She wasn't a coward. "I can't leave you here to face these jerks. They'll hurt the children again. And besides, you need help getting out of here first."

"Some of us can safely jump the stretch of distance to clear the stream and wall."

"But not enough of you to fight that entire pack. Leaving the others behind, especially the children, only gives the pack power over those of you who do manage to get out."

"I have no other plan, Tara."

"I'll think of something. Once I'm out of here." She had to decide what to do, and where she would go. She was too far from home —even if that was an option. Logan had said they were close to Damian's home. If he wasn't able to track her, could she find her way to Damian? How hard would it be to get to Riverside Park? Her car was still at the cabin, but Erik had said it wouldn't be safe to return there. She shook her head. She'd have to take the chance; she needed that car.

Senya talked her into resting until it was time to try and escape. The young female sat by the cave wall and had Tara lie down and rest her head in her lap. The exhaustion from the extensive healing weighed heavy on her and it was only a matter of minutes before she fell asleep.

She dreamed of Logan. Their precious night together replayed itself in her mind, and she relived every moment they had been together, every touch, every emotion. She woke up with his name on her lips. Her heart was heavy. Was he all right? Was he even now looking for her?

Just as Erik had said, the guards were noticeably less alert during their dinner break. They walked away from the cave's entrance and gave Tara the perfect chance for escape. She carefully stepped into the silver stream and then climbed over the three foot wall. She moved as quickly and as quietly as she could. With one last glance at the cave's entrance, she took off in a sprint to the east where Erik said there would be an opening in the back of the caves.

She paced herself, jogging slowly. Further in, the long narrow corridor of the dark cave's interior became blacker. It finally got to the point where she had to slow down to a careful walk when she couldn't see more than a few feet ahead of her. Even though the cave was cold, she was sweating.

How far back did this corridor lead? Would she be able to find the opening? The relentless doubts assailed her and she mentally scolded herself, *Stop it. I'm not afraid of the dark. I'm not afraid of caves. I got away without the guards noticing. So there's nothing to be worrying about.* But another question reared its ugly head: *How long do I have before they discover I'm missing from the other prisoners?*

She couldn't see her watch face so she wasn't sure how long she'd been walking. It felt like hours. Her eyes had become adjusted to the darkness and her confidence grew so she walked a little faster.

The narrow hall of the cave began to widen out. She rounded a bend in the path and came into a small open area. At first she couldn't see any opening, only surrounding walls. Then, a light touch of air caressed over her and she followed the direction it had come from. Across the circular area she found a small boulder propped against the cave wall. She could feel fresh air flowing around it. Thankfully, the boulder wasn't very big and after a little grunting and pushing she managed to move it back. Directly behind it was a small opening that led to the outside. Tara dropped to her knees and crawled through.

Outside she stood for a long moment trying to get her bearings. Being born in a Goddess worshipping family, she had been taught at an early age to read the night sky and stars. Her father had insisted that his children know everything there was to know about the Heavens and the Gods. Tara had never thought the knowledge would ever come in handy. *Thank you, father.*

The lake and the cabin lay in the west. She'd already made up her mind that she was going back, despite Erik's warning. She had to know if Logan was all right. She shook her head. *I won't think about him being hurt. I can't.*

Time was running out and that sense of urgency spurred her forward into the unknown area surrounding the caves. She kept her path going west, and only faltered a few times when the forest trees became too dense for her to see the stars.

What seemed like an eternity later, she stumbled out of the forest and saw the cabin in front of her. Her feet took on wings as she ran across the ground and burst into the cabin with Logan's name on her lips.

He wasn't there. She skidded to a halt in front of the stairs where she'd last seen him. Dried blood stained the wood floors where he had fallen, but there was no other indication that he'd even been there. Her heart sang with the jubilation that he had healed and was even now out there looking for her.

She hurried back outside to her car. Just as she reached to open the car door she realized that chances were Logan still had her car keys.

"Darn him and his macho stubbornness!"

She took a deep breath to calm down. Her logical mind reasoned out that Logan had no reason to trust her before, and keeping the car keys had kept her in his protective care. What was she going to do now?

She had no other options. She was going to have to go back and try to do something to help release the shifter prisoners. And she'd have to do it without Damian's help like she'd planned.

She jogged back to the forest. A tiny voice in the back of her mind told her that now was her chance to escape. She could hike into the nearest town and get help. She didn't have to risk her freedom by going back to the shifter caves. Logan would track her there, but he wouldn't be able to tell where she'd disappeared to afterwards because her scent would lead right to the cave. And, she added mentally, she was out of her mating cycle for the time being and that meant she'd have less chance of running into hunting shifters on her trail.

Just for the briefest moment, she hesitated.

Her heart won the battle over her head. She hurried into the concealing woods and back towards the cave. She couldn't run away —not from the shifters who needed her—or from Logan.

Logan. I wish you were holding me right now.

She didn't have any problems following the same path the Greek Pack had taken her earlier. Before too long she was back at the caves. She stayed hidden behind a large-trunk tree and surveyed the area. Several guards were still posted at the entrance to the big cave where the prisoners were, but she couldn't see anyone else.

The hair on the back of her neck rose. Were the others in their wolf forms and even now looking for her? What if they were closing in on her? Had they discovered her absence so soon? Her gaze flew around, searching every open area she could see, her heart racing with all the unanswered questions. And, where was Logan?

She resolutely ignored the nervous butterflies fluttering in her stomach. She had to think of a way to help the others escape. There were two guards, big burly men who looked like they could take down the biggest, toughest football player and still come out of the scuffle untouched.

She grinned. *I could always march up to them and demand that they obey me as their future Queen and release the prisoners.* Yeah, like that was going to work! But the more she thought about it, the better the idea seemed to be. She knew she couldn't physically best them, so why not mentally challenge them?

She had to take several deep calming breaths and slow exhales before she could force her feet to move forward. But when she stepped from the concealing protection of the woods, Tara Stuart walked with head high.

She walked straight up to the guards. Their expressions of complete shock and surprise would have been comical if she'd had the inclination to laugh.

"Don't look so shocked," she berated them with what she hoped was a regal tone. "What did you expect from a Goddess? Surely you weren't foolish enough to think you could contain me?"

It took a lot of willpower not to giggle at the words! She held their gaze and propped her hands on her hips for good measure. "Now, I demand that you release the prisoners." When they didn't move, she glared with regal disdain. "Don't just stand there staring at me like dumb bunnies! Do what I commanded. Now!"

One of the guards actually made the move to turn back into the caves. The other growled a protest. He shot a nasty look at her. "How the hell did you get past us?"

Tara shrugged nonchalantly. "That should be obvious. I am a Goddess, after all."

The two men exchanged looks. She could almost hear what they were thinking. They were worried that she was telling the truth, and they wondered just how dangerous she might be.

But a split second later one of the guards growled again. He glared at her. "You are not Queen yet, little human. And I have the feeling you have no more power than I do."

He lunged forward and grabbed her. Tara hadn't expected the movement and wasn't prepared. She screamed and kicked, trying to break free. He grabbed her by both arms and twisted them behind her back. She cried out with the wrenching pain as he jerked hard trying to pull her to the ground.

A ferocious roar broke over Tara's screams of protest. She looked up just in time to see a huge mountain lion lunge forward and take the other guard down.

Chapter Seventeen

"Logan!"

Just as the guard hit the ground, he instantly shifted into his wolf form. The lion and wolf tore into each other, teeth and claws, their ferocious battle cries deafening.

Tara fought like an enraged animal, too. She struggled against the guard's hold, kicking backward and landing hard blows to his legs. He yowled in pain and she managed to wrench free. She swung around to face him and gasped in shock. He shifted into his wolf form right before her eyes.

Uh oh. How am I supposed to fight him that way? She backed away, slowly, hands out in front of her in a defensive stance.

"Nice puppy," she cajoled softly. But he didn't take well to her tone. He bared his sharp canine teeth and advanced on her with a growl so nasty she shivered despite her bravado.

Tara bit back a gasp of dismay. Behind her she could hear the ferocious fight between Logan and the other guard still raging. She didn't dare call out for help and distract Logan, so what was she going to do?

Just then, that strange tingling started in her hands again. Holding them out in front of her she was startled to realize that she could actually see the glowing aura Senya had first noticed. "What the—"

The tingling was stronger this time. More heated. She felt a strange burning radiate from somewhere deep inside her—it felt like it came from the very depths of her soul and it rose with a surge so fast and so furious it left her gasping for breath. It surfaced from her, out through her hands, in a streak of flaring light. The arcing beam shot straight at the wolf striking him directly in the forehead.

He yowled painfully, the cry deafening, and then collapsed at her feet. Dead.

Tara stared in shock. Her entire body shook with the aftermath of residual energy. It was though she had projected her own energy into that stream of light, and it left her feeling depleted after leaving her body. What had just happened? She had just performed magick —and never knew she had that kind of power before then. Her knees gave out and she collapsed to the ground still shaking.

Suddenly the sound of the raging battle between Logan and the other wolf penetrated her fogged thoughts and she turned to look. The mountain lion was tearing the big wolf to shreds. Both animals were bleeding profusely in countless places on their bodies, but it was obvious that the lion was winning the battle. He had the wolf pinned to the ground as he swung his massive cat claws and sliced deep grooves into the wolf.

In a few more seconds, it was over. The wolf released one last howl of pain and rage and then slumped into a death sleep. The lion heaved a deep exhale of breath and stepped off the wolf. His body heaved with the battle's exertions and blood dripped from his wounds in a steady plop to the ground. He slowly lifted his head and turned to stare at Tara.

She barely managed to hold back her cry. Instead she bit down on her bottom lip. Logan's cat eyes shone with a fire that was fierce and bright. That look seared her to the very depths of her soul.

Before she could reason why, she was up and running to him. She reached him and fell to her knees beside him. "Logan," she whispered his name on a broken sigh, and wrapped her arms around his bulky lion's frame.

Logan shuddered. The action was rough and long and it shook Tara to her bones. She hugged him, unaware of the tears falling from her eyes.

"Are you all right?" She ran her hand lightly over the many bleeding wounds. Thankfully, they weren't as deep as she'd first suspected.

That is, until she touched the one by his left flank. He flinched and growled out in pain. Tara took her hand away and stared in horror at the gush of blood flowing from the deep wound. "Oh, Goddess!"

Before she could even think what to do, Logan suddenly slumped. She cried out as he fell unconscious to the ground.

Tara panicked, her thoughts flying in chaotic directions. Fear threatened to swamp her, body and mind. She'd never seen so much blood, and she wasn't even sure he was breathing! She finally managed to calm down enough to check for his pulse. It beat faint, but at least he was still alive. Thank the Goddess!

What did she do now? She looked at her hands. Could she heal him? Her hands trembled as she reached out and placed them gently over the gaping wound.

The tingling radiated out from her, stronger than ever before. It was as though her emotions and her feelings for this man was mixed in the heated energy and became a force that was indescribable.

Slowly the wound started to heal. Blood stopped flowing. The skin around the wound began to close, knit together with invisible thread. When it was over, all that was left was a long ragged, white scar.

Tara ran her hands gently over the rest of his wounds and healed them too. By the time she was finished she was ready to slump down beside him in total exhaustion. She leaned her head down to rest on the top of his. Logan was still unconscious and she was getting more worried by the minute. His wounds were healed—why wasn't he awake?

She lightly shook his shoulders. He didn't move. "Logan, please wake up now." But the big cat didn't respond.

Tara struggled to her feet. She needed help. And she had to act quickly, before the rest of the Greek Pack returned from where ever they had gone. She hurried back into the cave where the shifter prisoners were. Senya and Erik let out a shout of jubilation when they saw her. She hurried over to the wall, climbed over it and ran to them.

"Logan found us," she explained quickly. "The two guards are dead, but I don't know where the others are."

"Most likely hunting," Senya said.

"Or, they have gone to the pack in the south and plan to capture them too," Erik stated. "Those who support Damian's claim to be Ruler are being taken prisoner while those who oppose are being recruited."

"We have to get you all out of here," Tara said, "And I need help with Logan. He hasn't woken yet. I don't know what to do." She looked back at the wall and the silver stream. "We need to build a platform over it. Where would I get that kind of supplies?"

Erik nodded in agreement. "The best bet is to use a door frame, or something like that. I think you would have better chance of dragging it in here and getting it propped than you would if you tried to drag a heavy log large enough to span across the stream. The only trouble is that one of the few doors we have here is in a cave at the far end of this compound. It's too far for you to drag here."

Tara wasn't about to accept defeat this late in the battle. "I'll just have to figure out a way."

She followed Erik's directions to the cave that had a door inside for one of the rooms. Inside the simply decorated interior she stood staring at the door. Getting the hinges out wouldn't be so much a problem. It was how she was going to drag that piece of board all the way back to the other cave that had her worried.

With a couple of bumps, bruises and scrapes, she finally managed to get the door off its hinges and laid it down on the floor. "Now what?" Her gaze flew around the room looking for something to use. She groaned. This was a shifter's cave and she wondered just how much of the human world's amenities they used. She surveyed the bedroom. It had the basics, a few chairs, a small dresser, and a narrow bed.

Tara wondered briefly if Damian's pack lived like this. It was a simple way of life, and not as rustic and wild as she'd first believed the shifters to live. The thought made her shiver. She remembered hearing that Damian's pack preferred living in their wolf forms more often than they did their human ones. There was no way of guessing what type of living abodes they had. *I'll just have to adjust.* She pushed the uncomfortable thoughts away. She'd deal with it later ... when she had to.

Her gaze fell on the bed again. It was covered with a simple, thin coverlet. An idea hit. She could use the coverlet to slide the door on. After a few bungled attempts, in which she ended up landing on her butt twice when she tried to carry the door over to the coverlet, she realized that she would have better luck taking the cover to the door! Half an hour later, Tara was walking backward as she pulled, dragged, the makeshift litter with the door.

It took her almost another hour to drag the litter back to the cave where the shifters waited. By that time she was exhausted all over again and her breathing was harsh and catchy. She fell to her knees at the front of the cave and gulped air into her starved lungs.

She looked over at Logan. He was still in lion form and still unconscious. Her heart stuttered. Why hadn't he regained consciousness by now? A horrifying thought hit her. What if she had only healed the outside of the wound? Not knowing how this new power worked, she might have only went skin deep and stopped the bleeding ... but left the internal injury still intact. *Goddess, help.*

She struggled to her feet and stumbled over to Logan. Panic threatened to overwhelm her logical thinking. *What do I do? How do I make the power work and do what I need it to?*

She placed her hand on the white scar line. And then jerked it back with a cry of dismay. His skin was burning hot! "Logan, I'm so sorry! I didn't realize. Oh, Goddess, what do I do now?"

Tears blurred her vision and she blinked them away. She couldn't allow herself to give into this stubborn exhaustion and the thought-stealing fear. She had to be strong. Too many were depending on her right now. Logan was depending on her.

She reasoned out her options. They were too few for her peace of mind. She knew she would have to attempt to heal Logan again, this time concentrating on his internal injuries. She just prayed her newfound power would guide her, and work the way it was needed.

She placed both hands over the healed skin. The exhaustion that had taken hold of her body from doing too much in the past twenty-four hours weighed heavily on her. She closed her eyes and prayed for strength.

If ever in her life she had needed the Goddess, she needed Her now. She needed strength, power, and knowledge. She prayed harder, then, than she'd ever done before. She prayed with every ounce of humility in her.

If she couldn't heal Logan ...

If he died ...

Then she wouldn't want to live either. She couldn't.

From somewhere deep inside her the fire of healing power stoked again, coming to life and surging up from her soul. It burned her, using for fuel what little physical strength she had left. She concentrated on healing Logan from within, visualizing an invisible force flowing through his body and leaving strength and health in its wake.

As the healing fire burned stronger from her hands into Logan's body, her waning strength left her. Black dots swirled in front of her vision. A frightening lethargy eased over and within her like a warm blanket. In the back of her mind she knew she had pushed her limits; the exhaustion was taking complete control of her body.

Dizziness overwhelmed her and she swayed but managed to keep her hands on Logan. She felt cold and hot at the same time and her body shook uncontrollably. But still she forced the healing power out of her and into Logan as deep as she could visualize.

She suddenly felt Logan stir. She felt his sharp intake of breath as his body heaved upwards beneath her hands. Jubilation surged through her. She had done it! She knew he was now completely healed.

She wanted to tell him that she was so happy that he was all right. She wanted to tell him that draining her last drop of life force energy had been worth it. She wanted to tell him that she loved him. But the words wouldn't come.

Blackness swamped her and she felt herself falling forward. Her eyes closed against her will, and her breath whooshed from her body. Her last coherent thought was that she was sure she had to be mistaken when she heard Logan say,

"Damn it, Tara. How could you be so foolish?"

Chapter Eighteen

Logan carried an unconscious Tara securely in his arms. He wanted to shake her. He wanted to make her open her eyes and see just how angry he was. He thought of all the things he wanted to say to her, scold her about, but the one thing his heart and soul really wanted to shout wouldn't come forward.

After regaining consciousness he had discovered Tara slumped over, barely breathing, and sickly white. He panicked, thinking that she was hurt, and his hands flew over her body in search of injury. He tried to shake her awake but she fell forward into his arms like the proverbial rag doll. For just one terrifying moment he thought she was ... dead.

He roared his fear and rage into the night.

An answering howl echoed from the cave behind him. Logan turned, prepared to fight again. He took in the two dead guards, one with a gaping, burning hole in the center of his forehead, and the other torn to pieces. He remembered killing the one, but couldn't figure out what had happened to the other. The last thing he remembered was being terrified that the other wolf would kill Tara before he could finish the one he was fighting and get to her.

Another howl broke through his confused thoughts. It wasn't a battle cry. It was a seeking call. And it was coming from the cave. He was going to have to investigate. He lifted Tara in his arms and carried her away from the cave. He gently placed her on a small grass covered spot underneath a tree.

Logan lifted his head and sniffed the air. Good. There were no signs of other shifters for the time being. He felt he could safely leave her here for awhile. He headed back to the cave with determined strides.

He found the door on the makeshift litter by the cave's entrance. Inside he found the shifter prisoners. Erik and Senya greeted him with a shout.

He started to jump over the low wall but Erik stopped him with a warning about the silver stream. "I don't know if cat shifters are susceptible to silver, but be careful."

Logan shook his head. "It doesn't bother us." Oddly enough, copper was the cat shifters' bane. It was an unknown fact outside the cat shifter world and they preferred to keep it that way.

Erik explained what had happened. Senya was concerned for Tara and started wringing her hands when Logan told her where she was.

"She's used too much energy," Senya told him. "She healed all of us, and then dragged that door here. She was already exhausted when the Greek wolves brought her here. I don't like this unconscious state she's in now. We have a healer in our pack, but she is old." She turned and gestured for the healer, an older woman, to come forward. "I pray she can help Tara."

Logan didn't like what he was hearing. Tara's newly acquired healing powers came with a price. And now she had most likely pushed that limit to its max. She had risked her own health to help the shifters ...

And then to heal him again.

The knowledge did something to him he wasn't sure he wanted to face. His head tried to stay logical. But his heart, his soul, was crying out with the acknowledgement of the truth.

She could have run when she had the chance. He would have died without her healing, and she could have been far away before any of the other shifters even knew which direction to look for her in. Chances are she might have escaped completely.

But she had stayed. She had risked everything to come back and help the shifter prisoners. She had risked her life to come back and heal him.

Logan clenched his hands into fists. He wasn't going to let her sacrifices be for nothing. He wasn't going to let her die.

He could admit the truth now. She was his heart. His life. His soul.

She was his mate. He loved her.

•

The wolf healer worked on Tara for over an hour. Logan tried to concentrate on the task at hand—securing the cave to keep the children safe while the others prepared for battle—and not think about what was going on with Tara. Now that he had finally accepted what his heart and soul had been telling him for a long time, he had to figure out what he was going to do about it.

They gathered heavy stones and boulders and built a blocking barricade over the entrance to the cave. The children were left inside, and knew where the other opening was that Tara had escaped from. If the battle fared badly, then the children would leave by that opening and escape into the forest. The parents would face the Greek Pack and whatever enforcements they'd managed to get when the time came.

Tara had been left inside with the children. Logan didn't want to take the chance that she'd be vulnerable to attack. He grinned. When she regained consciousness and discovered she was back— almost a prisoner again in the cave—she was sure to be as mad as hell at him for putting there.

He just hoped she stayed put. If she was anywhere near the battle when it started she would only be a distraction he couldn't afford.

He didn't have long to dwell on those thoughts. The sentry guards Erik had placed near the forest's edge suddenly whined out the warning call. The Greek Pack was returning. Logan and the others were already in their shifter forms, ready for the attack.

When the Greek Pack sauntered out of the forest and into the clearing near the caves, Logan and the others surged forward. Chaos erupted. The battle was fierce and deadly.

•

Damian and Colin stood back to back. Their fur bristled and stood on end. Their canine teeth gleamed sharply white as their lips pulled back in snarls. They were trapped.

Damian knew the four men surrounding them were not shifters. Their smell was full human. Behind them, three other shifters—two of them Sinclair cousins—stood to the side in their wolf forms and waited.

The trap had been sprung so easily. Damian fumed at his own carelessness. When the female wolf had come to him and told him what she'd heard, he and Colin had immediately went in search of the two cousins. It was pure carelessness on their part that he and Colin didn't take note that the two wolves realized they were being followed and had led them away from the Pack's home and straight into an ambush. Whether or not the human men had been waiting for that reason or not, didn't matter. They took advantage of the situation and instantly surrounded Damian and Colin. They would have to fight for their lives to get out of this one, Damian knew. He just wasn't sure of the outcome.

"So, this is the alpha wolf of the pack and his sibling," one of the men stated in a satisfied tone. "What luck to capture them both at the same time."

"Make sure your guns have stun needles only," another man spoke up. "We don't want to damage them in any way."

Damn. Stun guns. Damian's hope sank that they would have a fighting chance. He mentally spoke to Colin, *We're outnumbered, Colin, but that doesn't mean we have to go down without doing some damage first.*

Agreed, his brother answered. *Let's take as much skin off these bastards as we can before they get us.*

Another mental voice spoke up, *Don't bother fighting, Damian. Save your strength.*

Damian snarled at his younger cousin, one of the wolves standing to the side, *You'll pay for your betrayal, Cruzel.*

Maybe, Cruzel grinned, his teeth showing, *but it won't be by your hands.*

Who is behind all this? Damian demanded. He wanted to know the name of the traitor who had instigated the uprising against his claim to the Wolven Throne.

Cruzel didn't answer. The humans moved closer and Damian and Colin braced themselves for attack. They never got the fighting chance. As one, the men raised their stun guns and fired. Instant blackness overtook his every sense and Damian fell. Colin fell by his side. Cruzel chuckled. Next step completed.

•

Tara waited, arms crossed and tapping her foot impatiently, for the last of the boulders to be removed from the cave's entrance. Behind her the wolf children howled in victory when they heard the voices of their parents assure them the battle was over and they were all safe.

She was going to kill Logan. When she had regained consciousness the wolf healer had told her what had happened. On one hand she was so thankful that Logan was healed completely. On the other hand, she was furious that he was out there fighting and could get injured again and she wouldn't be there to help him.

His was the first face she saw. Her heart swelled. She wanted to run into his arms. It took every ounce of willpower she had to stay where she was as she stared at him and tried to figure out what that strange expression on his handsome features meant. His eyes glowed dark blue fire, and starkly hungry. She lost her breath and all coherent thoughts. She trembled, afraid all the love she felt for him was shining in her eyes and he was seeing it. She didn't care. She loved him and she always and forever would. No matter what happened now.

He strode up to her and stopped a few inches away. She felt the familiar heat that always seemed to radiate off him touch her and she shivered. She wanted him to hold her.

"Are you all right?" he asked in a deep husky tone.

She nodded. "Is it over?" Her gaze searched him over from head to toes. "You're not hurt, are you?"

"No."

He was staring at her with that strange look. She just couldn't decide if it was anger for some reason or if … it was the same look he had when he'd made up his mind to make love to her the night before. She hoped it was the latter.

Tara glanced around at the other shifters. They were gathering up their children to take back to their caves. Every one of the adults had some injury or another. The battle had been deadly, she was sure. She didn't want to think what the battle field looked like; dead wolves everywhere and blood drying on the ground.

"How many are hurt?" she asked Logan. "I can help."

To her surprise he growled, the sound nasty and rough. "You dare lay a hand on any of them and I'll turn you over my knees and beat you."

Shocked, she stared at him, not believing he had threatened her like that. "But—"

"This isn't open for debate, Tara," he growled out another rough expletive. "You've used too much healing power. What the hell were you thinking? Didn't it occur to you that when you were using that power your life energy was being drained? Or were you stupidly ignoring that weakness?"

"Stupidly?" she sputtered. "Did you just call me stupid?" She wanted to hit him. "That's the thanks I get for saving your life?"

"I didn't ask you to."

"You were unconscious and dying! What choice did I have?"

The fire in his eyes blazed to life again. "You could have chosen not to. It certainly would have solved a lot of your problems right now if I'd died."

"You arrogant beast!" She didn't stop to think—she hit him in the chest with both open hands. Just for good measure, simply because he acted as though her strike hadn't bothered him at all—she struck again. Hard. "I can't believe you just said that. Do you really believe that I would just walk away and let you die? Do you, Logan?" She spun away to angrily pace back and forth, waving her hands and glaring at him every time she turned in his direction. "I should have! I had the perfect chance to escape, and instead I let my heart rule my head and I stayed. I could have been miles away right now. Instead, I'm here, exhausted beyond belief, and listening to you scold me because I did a good deed. You're right. I'm stupid."

"I didn't call you stupid." Logan grabbed her by both arms as she marched past him. She struggled for a minute until he finally shook her and glared sternly. "You scared the hell out of me, Tara. I didn't know to what extent your healing power had drained you. I didn't even know if you were strong enough to recover from using it. I've seen healers die from using too much, too soon."

"I didn't die."

His groan was half growl. "No thanks to your heart ruling you instead of your head."

What was he really saying? Tara felt like she couldn't catch her breath and her heart beat fast. "Is that such a bad thing?"

Logan stared down into her face, his expression hard to read. "This time, maybe it was."

She had to know. "Because I'm your responsibility until you deliver me to Damian?"

"Yes."

Her heart broke. Even after the night they had shared, hearts and souls mingling, he thought of her as only an obligation. Her heart didn't want to accept the truth, but her head knew it for what it was. Tears stung her eyes but she blinked them back. Not for anything would she let him see how much his words hurt. How much it was killing her to realize and accept that what she felt for him would never be returned. He was right. She was stupid. Foolish.

She took a deep breath. With a hard jerk she twisted free from his grasp. If she was going to survive this, if she was going to accept her destined future, then she would do it with as much pride as she possessed.

She lifted her head and their gazes locked. "As you've stated, Logan, I'm nothing more than a responsibility to you. But that doesn't mean you have the right to tell me what I can or can't do. I'm going to check with Erik and Senya and find out if anyone needs healing. Don't look so furious. This is my choice and you have no say in it. You have no rule over me. I can use whatever energy I choose to."

"Try it and I'll—"

"Don't you dare threaten me!"

"I'm not threatening," he murmured silkily. "I'm promising."

Stalemate. A thrill of fear ... and something more intense hit her, spiraling through her body like a rushing wave of potent desire and adrenaline. She had the feeling that pushing Logan any further would result in a situation that neither of them would fare well from.

She didn't care. She pushed anyway. She turned to walk away. "You can wait for me in the clearing. I don't know how long it will take to heal them all but—ahh! Logan!"

Her regal speech ended on a scream as he lunged forward and grabbed her from behind. Before she could even finish her squeal of protest, he bent and hefted her over his shoulders. Hanging face down over his shoulders she pounded on his back and struggled with every ounce of energy she had left in her.

"Let me go, you beast! Logan, put me down!" She tried kicking but he held her legs down with one arm, effectively keeping her from doing him any harm, and he stomped into a nearby cave.

Tara had never said a foul word in her life. But she had heard plenty of them, especially from the man carrying her like a sack of potatoes, and so she furiously spat out every one she could remember, raining them down on Logan as she pounded on his back.

He ignored the words and her struggles. A few moments later he suddenly stopped and flipped her over his shoulders to drop her onto a soft surface. Tara hit the mattress with an indignant "oomph!" and pushed her hair out of her eyes. She stared up at Logan in shock.

He grinned at her. She couldn't believe his audacity and told him so with a few more choice words.

"You don't even know what half those words mean," he said softly, his voice deep.

"I hate you."

"No you don't."

No, she didn't. But she wanted to. It would make things so much easier if she could just force her heart to forget what she really felt for him. "I want to," she admitted in a whisper, her very heart in those words, loud and clear.

Logan's grin disappeared. He ran a hand over his face and closed his eyes for a long moment. "What would it take, angel? Tell me what I can do that would make you stop looking at me like that. You need to hate me." He groaned. "For both our sakes. You need to hate me."

Tara couldn't stop the words. She didn't even want to. No matter what happened, she had to tell him.

"I can't hate you, Logan." She bit back a cry of dismay. "I love you."

He was so still. His handsome features were etched in stark hunger. His eyes blazed an blue fire that threatened to scorch her. For the rest of her life Tara would remember that look on his face after she had said the words that would change everything between them.

"No, you don't." Logan frowned. He turned away from her. "You don't love me, Tara. It's just the aftereffects of all we've been through together these past few days. You're exhausted and you're emotionally drained. And right now I'm looking like some kind of hero in your eyes. When I finally get you safely to Damian, all this will seem like some kind of bad dream and you'll forget about me."

Did he really believe that? She didn't know whether to be hurt or angry. She chose angry. She knew he had felt something when he'd made love to her. He couldn't have loved her like he had and not felt something for her other than just lust. It hadn't been her cycle that had forced him to give in to his basic desires. He had wanted to make love to her. And now he was telling her to hate him and forget him.

"You're a coward, Logan Cross."

He growled dangerously and swung back to face her. "Careful, angel. You may think you know what you're doing, but you're too naïve, too innocent. You're going to get hurt if you continue with this."

"I'm already hurt," she whispered. "I know you're going to walk away from me." She pushed to her feet and faced him, their bodies mere inches apart. "But no matter what you do or say, Logan, I could never hate you."

"Try harder."

"Jerk! Why are you being this way?"

"Because I have enough sense in me to realize that this is crazy, Tara. We are just a few hours away from Damian's home, and he's expecting us any time now. I only wanted to give you time to rest before we left here."

Anger surged. If he wanted to walk away from whatever it was between them, then she'd let him. She refused to beg. "Fine. I'll rest for a few minutes and then we can leave. No need for you to be burdened with me any longer than you have to be."

"You're twisting my words," he muttered. "You should have been a redhead instead of a blonde; it suits your temperament better."

"Keep up the insults and I'll be the one growling instead of you!"

"Damn it, Tara. Will you just shut up, and rest? You're going to be the death of me."

Now, why had her outburst caused him to become angrier? "You don't like the idea of me growling?"

"You're human, angel. I don't like the idea of you sounding like a damn wolf shifter and growling like one, too."

She held back her grin. "You're a damn cat shifter and you growl."

"I bite, too."

Chapter Nineteen

That was the most sensual threat she'd heard from his mouth. She couldn't help it. She smiled at him. "I know."

The air between them arced with invisible, electrical tension. Tara was sure Logan could hear the too-fast beating of her heart in the silence that cloaked them, cocooning them in the small space.

Her hands shook as she reached up and pulled aside her hair off her left shoulder. The collar of her blouse was low enough for her to push it down and bare her shoulder and the top of her breast to his smoldering gaze. She ran her hands over the spot on the upper curve of her back shoulder where he had bit and marked her during their lovemaking. She could still feel the slight ridge where his teeth had sunk, marking her forever.

"Do all shifters mark their—partners—when they make love?"

"No." He growled the word out as if it had been forced through clenched teeth.

"When?"

Logan made a choking sound and cleared his throat. "When what?"

"When do they mark them? Do they ever mark a partner … instead of a mate?"

"Stop this, Tara," he warned, his voice deep and rough.

"Tell me, and I won't ask any more questions."

Logan shook his head. She didn't have a chance to even protest before he suddenly reached out and lifted her in his arms. He had her down on the mattress in mere seconds. He released her and rolled over to her side. "Don't. Say. Another. Word." He emphasized each word with an angry clip. "Rest."

She wanted to argue. She needed to hear the truth. For both their sakes, she needed to know ...

But instead she shut her mouth. Then, with one last look into his stormy eyes, she shut her eyes. Her heart ached, but she knew Logan wasn't going to say any more. *You win, Logan. Goddess help me, but I wish I could hear you say the words I so desperately need to hear. How can I face the future, married to another man that I don't love, and never have even the comfort of knowing you cared about me?*

She felt hot tears burn behind her closed lids. To keep him from seeing them, she turned her back on him and pretended to sleep. Minutes later she drifted off, his name whispering in her mind and her heart hurting so much that she knew she'd never recover from the pain.

•

Erik, Senya and a few of the other males decided to go with Logan and Tara the final stretch of the journey. Their pack had decided to merge with Damian's in his territory, but the move would take some time.

Erik felt the extra protection for Tara could be used in case there were other packs like the Greeks waiting to ambush the others that sided with Damian's rule. Logan didn't comment or disagree but Tara thought he was most likely relieved that they wouldn't be making the last lap of the trip together ... alone. He hadn't spoken to her since she had woken from her rest and found him gone. She'd found him with Erik. He'd glanced at her but seemed to be avoiding looking directly at her.

She refused to let it hurt her any more than it already was. She helped Senya gather up some needed herbs for the Healer so that she would be well stocked, and then she spent a few minutes saying goodbye to the children. Some of them had tears in their eyes; their awe of her was still apparent, and she couldn't get past the fact that they already seemed to worship her as their Queen. It was disconcerting.

She didn't want to be Queen. She wanted to run away from her destined fate and forget the world of shifters ever existed. Forget that she had fallen in love with one.

They went back to the cabin and got the car. The four other males who had volunteered to go with them went ahead on foot in wolf forms to scout the area. They could reach the Park faster with their preternatural speed.

Two hours later, Logan turned off the Interstate and drove to Riverside State Park. He slowed the car and pulled into the large parking area. He drove through, leaving the public area and then onto a narrow dirt road that led off into the woods. He parked the car near where the road ended abruptly in front of a small clearing where a hiking path could be seen.

"Damian's pack lives about two miles further into the woods," he explained in a monotone voice. "They're in an isolated spot up against a mountain. Their home caves are there."

Erik nodded his head in understanding. "Far enough off the beaten path to be away from the humans who hike in this area."

"They've been lucky," Logan said. "Riverside Park is a popular spot, but none of the pack members have ever been exposed in all the decades they've been here."

Senya walked at Tara's side while Logan led and Erik followed behind them as a rear guard. Both males were on full alert, ready for anything. They constantly sniffed the air, and listened for even the slightest off-sound. They saw no sign of the other four wolf males but knew that they were already scouting ahead; they'd left a scented sign at the beginning of the trail.

Two miles further in the woods, Logan stopped and motioned for them to stay still and silent. He spoke on the mental path of shifters to Erik and Senya. *There should be sentry guards here from Damian's pack. I don't even sense your males. We're too close to the dens and we haven't spotted a wolf yet. Something's not right.*

Tara knew something was wrong; she could tell by the way Logan's body tensed as if ready for a fight. Senya placed a hand on her arm and whispered, "Tara, Logan thinks something is amiss. Stay close to me."

Logan motioned for Erik to scout back the way they had come. The man shifted instantly into his wolf form and glided like a fleeting shadow into the woods behind them. Logan nodded his head to Senya who nodded back and then he changed into his lion form. Ears lying back against his large head, eyes narrowing, tail swishing, he slowly moved forward.

Senya turned to Tara. "Would you feel more comfortable if I stayed in human form?"

Tara watched Logan disappear into the woods ahead of them.

"If you feel the need to be in wolf form, it won't bother me," she answered. "What's wrong?"

"We don't sense any other wolves around. Logan says we should be near Damian's sentry guards now. He and Erik have decided to scout out the area. We need to wait here for them. If something happens—don't worry, I'm sure everything is okay—but should something happen I will shift to my wolf form to protect you. Stay always behind me, as close as possible."

Tara shivered. Her active imagination ran wild with the scenarios that could happen if something was wrong like Logan felt. Would this be the way it was, for the rest of her life among these shifters? Always afraid for her life, always having to face a battle? Could she adjust?

Erik suddenly appeared out of the woods and walked to them, changing as he came. "The path behind us is clear. There are no recent scents other than ours. How long has Logan been gone?"

"About fifteen minutes."

Just as Senya finished answering Logan in cat form came jogging out of the woods in front of them. He didn't bother to change as he trotted up to Erik. Tara could tell they were mentally communicating and she put it down to something else she should have known about shifters.

Senya touched her arm. "Logan says there are human scents mixed with wolf shifters in an area just ahead. He wants you to stay here while we investigate. Our males' scents are mixed with the others, so whatever is going on is there." Senya glanced at Logan and grimaced before looking back at Tara but avoiding direct eye contact with her. "He says ... uh ... for you not to be stubborn and argue about this. He said 'I can still give you a spanking before turning you over to Damian if you disobey me.'"

Tara fumed. She glared at Logan. "Disobey me? Logan, you are the most arrogant man." She put her hands on her hips. "And, as for giving me a spanking, you just wish you could. Ha, you wouldn't dare. So, guess what? I'm not afraid. Go on, do what you have to do and I'll stay right here. That's my choice, just so we're straight on that."

Logan growled, his cat eyes narrowing to slits. Senya gasped at the angry sound. "Tara, I can't repeat what he just said."

"I can guess," Tara muttered. She deliberately turned away from him and walked over to a small boulder and sat. "Hurry back. I'm ready to get this journey over with."

Logan hissed, growled one last nasty threat, then stalked away. Erik and Senya changed to wolves and followed. Tara closed her eyes for a long minute. When she opened them, the three shifters were gone.

She hadn't meant that last statement. She really didn't want to be so close to her new life. But most of all, she didn't want to part on such bad feelings between her and Logan. She wanted to remember nothing more than the night he'd marked her and made love to her, claiming her heart and soul forever. That precious memory would last a lifetime.

And help get her through a long life married to another man.

•

Logan slinked low to the ground and came to a stop. Erik and Senya copied his movement. They were positioned atop a huge boulder that looked down into a small clearing surrounded with other large boulders. Below them they could see what was going on. Four men surrounded the two huge wolves, Damian and Colin. Both wolves were lying unconscious on the ground. Three other wolves stood to the sides.

Why the hell are humans involved in this mess? Logan demanded mentally.

Erik grunted under his breath. "We heard Colin had been attacked by a lone outside-the-pack wolf shifter and had human help. Too, Damian has been suffering a strange illness that his Healer can't fix. It's been rumored that the shifters wanting to stop Damian's rule might have human help. Why the humans would be involved is the mystery. There can't be any gain in helping. At least, not that any of us can surmise."

"Someone—a shifter—has promised them something. Something very important." Senya commented. "But having humans involved is more than just dangerous. It's suicidal. We're all at risk."

Logan surveyed the scene below and murmured. "I hope Damian and Colin are only unconscious." The men carried guns but he couldn't detect a blood scent from either of the wolves. Most likely, the men had used tranquilizers. Still, that didn't mean the men didn't carry bullets, too. He looked the other three wolves over, calculating their strengths and sizes. Three of them: one each for him, Erik, and

Senya. Somehow they would have to get the men away from the unconscious wolves.

Or kill them.

"We can ambush the other shifters. But we need to dispose of the humans first. Senya, head toward the east, leaving a clear trail. Stay just ahead of the shifters but keep them following you no matter what. Give us ten minutes, then hide your trail and get back here." Logan watched the female wolf slink quietly away. He turned to Erik. "Chances are the humans are going to be on alert when the shifters leave to follow Senya. To confuse them, I'll come in one direction and you come in opposite of me. Make as much of a ferocious noise as you can. Howl, growl, stomp, tear up shrubs as you advance."

Erik moved away, quickly disappearing into the surrounding shrubs. Logan watched as the three shifters below suddenly caught scent of Senya, and with growls they left the clearing to investigate.

A few minutes later, Erik started his advance into the clearing, making enough noise to scare even the strongest human. Logan had to give the wolf credit. He sounded like he had a small army of wild wolves with him. The men nervously looked around, trying to figure out what was going on and in what direction the threat was coming from. Even though they held their guns up and ready, Logan noticed that they didn't reload. It was a lucky break for him and Erik. Hopefully it meant they wouldn't have to be dodging bullets.

Logan stood on the boulder. Just as Erik charged into the clearing, he jumped. Flying through the air he landed on the first two men standing close together. Out of the corner of his eyes he saw Erik lunge forward and plow into the other two men. And to his surprise he saw the other four shifter wolves from Erik's pack erupt from the bushes and join in the battle.

It was over in a matter of minutes. Logan and the wolves were unscathed, but the four men were torn to shreds. *It is better this way*, Logan thought. Leaving behind humans who could tell others about them wasn't smart. He just hoped they were the only ones involved in this mess. He'd have to have his Cat Council look into the possibilities that other humans were infiltrating the shifter world and for what purpose. It didn't bode well to ignore any of this.

Just as they were about to try and revive Damian and Colin, the other three wolves that had followed Senya now burst back into the clearing. They skidded to a halt and stared at Logan, Erik and the other four.

Welcome back, Logan drawled mentally. *Care to join your human friends?*

They lifted their muzzles in snarls but remained silent. Senya came into the clearing and changed back to human form. She knelt down beside Damian and Colin.

"They're both still unconscious. Here are the tranquilizer darts they used." She pointed to the darts still protruding from the left flanks of both males. She started to pull them out. Erik stopped her.

"Careful, love. They may be poisoned."

Senya chewed on her bottom lip in consternation. "I think you're right. It looks like an infection is already starting around the edges where the darts went in. We need to get them to the Healer as soon as possible."

The four wolf males from Erik's pack caged in the three rogues and forced them to march out. Logan and Erik changed back to men and picked up Damian and Colin.

"Senya, retrieve Tara and bring her to the dens. They are located about a half mile from where she is, direct west."

Damian's body was a dead weight in Logan's arms. The wolf shifter was a big man but lean, so his wolf form shouldn't have been so heavy. Logan had the bad feeling that whatever poison had been used in those darts was quickly stiffening the wolf's body ...

... Preparing it for death.

Chapter Twenty

Tara reached Damian's compound before Logan did, and was waiting impatiently for him. Senya had told her that he and the wolves had taken care of the humans without getting hurt but she had to see for herself that he was really all right.

A lovely, mature woman named Emily greeted Tara and Senya when they arrived. One of the wolf males from Erik's pack had already arrived to explain what had happened and Damian's sentry guards hurried out to meet the two women. The guards had just returned from searching for Damian and Colin but had been scouting the area to the north. They returned to the dens right before the women and then was told the news. Emily welcomed Tara and Senya warmly and saw to their comfort as they waited for the men to bring Damian and Colin back.

Senya and Emily conversed but Tara couldn't sit still long enough to join the conversation. She kept up a steady pace by the front entrance of Damian's cave where they waited and she tried hard not to appear too overly anxious.

Finally Logan and the others returned. Seeing Logan carrying the big grey wolf, Emily let out a choked cry and hurried forward. Tara rushed to Logan's side.

"Are they alive?" she asked in a whisper.

Logan nodded his head. "Yeah. So far. Whatever they had in those tranquilizer darts is poisoning them."

Another woman came hurrying out of a cave and rushed over to the men. Emily quickly introduced her as the Healer Rose. She immediately checked Damian and Colin and then told the men to carry them to Damian's cave.

Inside, Rose went to work trying to save Damian and Colin's

lives. Emily stood at her side, ready to help if needed. Tara watched the healer in action, amazed that she was using the same technique she had when she'd heal Logan and the others. The woman placed both hands on Damian's head, closed her eyes, and concentrated. Even from where she stood, Tara could see the faint aura of healing energy as it flowed from the woman's hands into the wolf's body.

But nothing happened. Rose sat in that position for almost an hour before suddenly slumping over in total exhaustion. Tara's heart raced. Damian hadn't even stirred. Was he going to die? She looked from Rose's face to the tear filled gaze of Emily. She could see the truth in their eyes.

What would happen if Damian died? And Colin, too? Would the Prophecy be changed to fit the needs of another ruling Prince of the Wolf packs? Would she still be destined to be the mate of that chosen Prince? She couldn't stop the shudder that wracked through her at the thought.

She didn't want to be mated with Damian. But she didn't want him to die, either. Tara searched her conscience. She had healing power. Some deep inner wisdom told her that she could heal Damian and Colin. She didn't know what the price would be, but she knew that she had no choice. Her conscience wouldn't let her just walk away when she knew that she could save his life. No matter what the consequences were after she did so.

I have to do this. I can't leave knowing that I was his only chance. She took a step forward.

Logan's hand gripped her upper arm in a strong hold that was painful. "Don't even think it," he warned under his breath. "If you expulsed that much healing energy it would kill you."

She turned back to look at him. "I have to do this, Logan. I'm the only one that can."

"Damn it, Tara. I won't let you risk your life like this. We'll give the healer time to rest and she can try again."

Tara shook her head. "She can't do it. I have to."

Logan growled low, his voice harsh, "If I have to carry you out of here and fight every wolf to do it, I will. I won't let you give your life for his."

"It's my choice."

Her whispered, heartfelt words echoed in the small cave. The tension radiating between them was so thick it felt suffocating.

Their gazes locked. Tara searched for something in his dark blue eyes, something she needed to know. She loved this man, this shifter who had stolen her heart from the very beginning and who even now was fighting to protect her.

But ... what did he feel for her? Was it only his possessive nature still being in protective mode? Or dare she hope that his feelings went much deeper?

She wanted to ask him, but the words wouldn't come. Not here, with Damian lying at Death's door and all his pack standing nearby. The moment passed and she felt it like a vicious stab to her heart. Even her soul cried out.

She gently pried Logan's hand away from her arm. They both knew that moment of truth, of acceptance. A sense of calm settled over Tara. She was ready to move forward.

Logan hissed under his breath. His blue eyes glowed with an inner fire as he stared at her. "This is goodbye, Tara," he said roughly. "I won't stay and watch you kill yourself."

Before she could open her mouth to protest, he turned away and stomped out of the cave. He never looked back.

Hot tears flooded her eyes. She couldn't believe that he'd just left her. Forever. She wanted to cry out his name, beg him to come back. But she knew it was for the best. She belonged here now and he belonged back in his world. No matter how desperately she wanted it, nothing could change their destinies.

Tara blinked away the tears and turned back to the healer still slumped over next to Damian. *I can do this. Everything will be all right. I know it.*

She instructed two of the men to help Rose to her feet and back to her own cave. She turned to find Emily at her side. The woman's face was drawn, shadows haunting her eyes. Tara felt the urgent need to comfort her and reached out to touch her shoulder.

"I can heal him, don't worry."

"We don't know what's wrong," Emily told her. "He's been ill for a long time now."

"Senya thinks someone was poisoning him all along. Then, whatever was used in the dart just added to that effect."

Emily paled. "What if it's too late?"

Tara refused to give in to that doubt. She patted Emily's arm reassuringly. Taking a deep calming breath she then exhaled slowly and sat down beside Damian.

She ran her hands softly over the furred body. A fevered heat radiated off him, intense in the invisible waves. She closed her eyes and centered her hands over his head. She felt energy heat slowly pass from her hands but it wasn't the beforehand strength she had known. Keeping her eyes closed, she calmed her mind and sought out the answer. Within moments, she knew that she needed to place her hands on Damian's stomach. The poison had settled there.

She concentrated, focusing all her strength and positive thinking into forcing out the healing energy she knew she possessed. A deep shudder rose from within her and pulsed out through her hands. The shock wave of healing energy was potent enough to wrench a gasp from her. She opened her eyes and saw the glowing light from her hands slowly penetrating the fur and going into Damian's internal body.

It was the most incredible feeling she'd ever experienced. It was also the most frightening.

And the most exhausting.

Tara knew when the healing energy finally located and struck at the poison in Damian. She felt it through the extreme tingling of her hands—as though her hands were suddenly going numb. As the energy strengthened within Damian it also drained from her. She could feel the relentless pull of her life force from the very depths of her soul. But she couldn't stop. She had to do this, no matter what.

Blackness swirled in her vision, tingling numbness spread over her entire body, and a sickening weakness flowed over her and through her. Damian became stronger. She was getting weaker.

The wolf stirred beneath her healing hands. She heard cries of joy behind her. She was so sleepy. *If I could just rest for a moment—*

The last coherent thought Tara had as the blackness claimed her was of Logan. Desperate, frightened, heartsick, and weary beyond belief, she called out his name, "Logan," and fainted.

•

She walked in fields of intense colors—greens, blues, reds and yellows. There were flowers everywhere, and the air carried a sweet calming scent of incense. There was a strange calmness deep inside her, a feeling of finally coming "home" but she wasn't sure where she was.

Where was Logan? And the others? This place didn't resemble

what she remembered of Damian's home. The last thing she could remember was the sickening exhaustion overwhelming her and then blackness. So, how had she ended up here?

"You *are* home, dear one," a voice whispered softly.

Tara looked up and saw a tall woman approach her. She walked as though she was floating on air, her gossamer gown flowing in invisible wind, her long silver hair flying back from a face that was sculpted beyond any beauty known to man.

"Goddess Azina." Tara immediately dropped to her knees in a curtsy.

Azina reached out and lifted Tara to her feet. She touched her cheek with a soft caress that left gentle tingles in its path. "Welcome, dear Tara."

"Why am I here? Did I die?"

Azina shook her head, her smile soft and kind. "No, child. Not yet. But you are close to death in the real world. Your body lies unresponsive. You are here in spirit with me for awhile."

Tara couldn't figure out why, but she didn't like the sound of that. "For how long?"

"That would depend on you. If you wish to return to your earthly body, I can make it so. If you wish to stay here, then it will be. The choice is yours. I know how unhappy you have been with the pre-destined fate that was put upon you. I have watched you through the years and my heart has felt your sadness.

"But I have chosen you … and the others … for a special reason, Tara. You are my daughters, direct descendents, and only through you can my shifter races be made strong against what is to come in the future. Your powers will be immense. You will rule by the shifter Princes and give them what they need to strengthen their people. Your children will do the same."

Tara felt the conviction in her heart and her soul. But she couldn't accept it. She didn't want to rule by Damian's side. She loved Logan. Tears burned her eyes.

"I can't love Damian."

"You love Logan."

"Yes." And it was a love that would live forever. Even if she didn't.

"I can give you a choice, my child, but I can not interfere in what's to be. You can choose to live. Or to die."

Tara bit back the instant response that sprung to mind. She would willingly choose death if it meant she wouldn't have to face life without Logan.

But she was needed. She knew that truth now. Her destiny was to rule and save lives. Could she allow her own selfish wants and needs to overrule that of her conscience, and fail all those who were depending on her for survival?

"I can't leave them," she choked out. She angrily wiped the tears from her eyes. "I want to be selfish, but I can't."

Azina smiled. "That is why you were chosen, Tara. Your soul is pure and unselfish."

Tara sighed. "I'm ready to go back now. If I dare stay here any longer I might—"

Azina touched her cheek again. "Then, so be it. Return to your destiny, Tara. And know that it is what was meant to be, no matter how hard the journey there was."

Tara took one last, long look at the Goddess. She memorized every feature on that incredibly beautiful face. "Thank you," she said. And she knew that she meant it.

•

She woke to the feel of familiar hands caressing her face. She opened her eyes. And stared straight into the face of her sister Mara.

"Mara?" She closed her eyes then reopened them again. Tara sat up in the bed she was lying in. "What are you doing here?" She glanced quickly around the room and recognized it as the cave she'd been in when attempting to heal Damian. Why was her sister here?

Mara hugged her. "I'm so glad you're awake. We were all very worried."

"How long was I unconscious?"

Mara sighed. "Too long. It's been six days."

"What?" Tara ran a shaky hand over her face. The deadening weakness was gone and she actually felt energized. Her moments with the Goddess seemed like a fading dream. But she was still very much confused.

"We thought you were going to die," Mara told her.

"I thought so, too."

"How do you feel?"

"Fine, actually." Tara looked closer at her sister. She was beautiful.

Radiant. Smiling happily. "Why do you look so happy? I realize you were worried about me, but it's something else isn't it? Something that has you glowing with happiness. Spill, Mara."

Her sister actually blushed. So unlike Mara. "I am happy, Tara. I can't believe this. I never expected it and everything was so sudden."

"You're making my head ache with this confusion."

"Sorry!" Mara laughed. "Okay, here's the full story in a nutshell. It turns out I was also chosen to mate with a Prince shifter. Colin. Damian's brother. The Goddess came to me and told me everything. She told me to come here as soon as possible. I had no idea where you were since you'd left home without telling us where you were going. When I arrived here I found you in a coma and the Wolf Prince preparing for a war."

"Oh no," Tara murmured. "Please tell me we're not about to be in the middle of a shifter war. I don't think I can take much more bloodshed."

"Don't worry, everything is fine now. Well, as fine as it can be considering the circumstances. Damian and Colin were set to rain hellfire down on their enemies but a Cat shifter contacted them and told them he had taken care of the band of human infiltrators and the shifter renegades."

"A cat shifter?" Tara's heart beat increased. Was it Logan?

"Apparently he is Prince over the cat shifter clans here in the U.S., and he sent a team of his own pack out to search out and destroy this band that was planning to take over control of all the shifters. Colin says he is a ruthless ruler and that if he says the threat has been contained then we can rest assured that it has. Impressive, huh?"

"Yes. Did Colin say who this shifter was?"

"Logan Cross."

Logan had come to the rescue again, one last time. Not only had he saved her life several times, but also Damian's and Colin's, and possibly a lot more shifters, too.

Tara's heart sank. She would never see him again. Could she bear it? The way her soul cried out told her that she would live her life loving a man she could never again be with.

Mara convinced her to eat a light meal and then she went back to sleep. Damian was going to come visit her later that evening and she wanted to be stronger when he did.

She slept, and she dreamed of Logan.

•

He was a handsome man, though a bit older than she expected. His dark hair was peppered with grey, but his body was still lean and strong. He sat down on the edge of the bed and they looked at each other for a long moment.

"Mara says you are better," Damian said in his deep voice.

"Yes. I'm thankful to see that you are, too."

"Thanks entirely to you. I was dying even before those bastards shot that poisoned dart into me. You healed me completely."

"I'm glad I was able to." What more could she say to get past this awkward first meeting? She searched his face, noting that his dark grey eyes were shadowed. She might as well get this over with and face what was to be. "What happens now? Do we marry right away?"

"Whenever you feel up to the ceremony," Damian answered, and then added softly, "And the mating."

Tara bit back a gasp. Could she go through this? Could she allow another man to touch her? Her heart and soul belonged to Logan. She wasn't sure she could do this after all.

She decided that the best thing to do was tell Damian the truth. She didn't want to start their lives together with lies and heartache haunting them. She took a deep breath and then met his gaze.

"Damian, I have to tell you something. Please believe that I don't want to hurt you. But, I need you to know that my heart and soul belongs to another man. Another shifter. I will carry through my end of this destiny but I can never be in love with you. I can't give you what belongs to him."

"I do understand, Tara," Damian admitted with a quiet sigh. "I feel the same way for another woman."

How sad was this? She couldn't believe that they each loved someone else and yet were unable to do anything about it. "How are we going to handle this," she asked, "when we feel this way?"

Damian was quiet for a long time. Tara watched his handsome features as he appeared deep in thought. She knew the exact moment when he made his decision. His eyes lighted up. He smiled disarmingly.

"Mara tells me you've been a rebel all your life."

Tara felt her cheeks heat. "I guess so. I just didn't like the idea that I would one day be forced to rule a shifter race by the side of a man I wouldn't love."

"Was it the *man* part of the destiny that bothered you most, because you wanted to choose your own mate? Or was it the *ruling* part?"

"Both."

"Would you give up the chance to rule as a Queen if you had the choice?"

Startled, Tara stared at him. What was he saying? Why did she suddenly feel so incredibly happy? She forced herself to calm down and ask, "If I had the choice? I'm sorry, Damian, but the truth is that I would give it up. I don't want to rule by your side as Queen."

Damian chuckled. "Well, that sounded honest enough." He touched her chin with a gentle caress. "Is this other shifter worthy of your love and devotion?"

Tara shrugged. "I don't even know how he really feels about me. But it doesn't matter anyway. We all have our destinies to fulfill. Mine is with you. Not him."

"Have you ever seen the Goddess Azina, Tara? Ever spoken to her?"

Tara was startled by the odd question. "Yes. In fact it was just recently. She gave me the choice to live or die."

"I spoke to her, too. These past six days while you hovered at Death's door, I prayed harder than I've ever done in my life." Damian stood up and paced a few feet from the bed. "You willingly risked your life to save mine. I couldn't believe that anyone could be so selfless. I knew then that you would make the perfect Queen to rule at my side."

He stopped pacing and turned to face her. "But I had already decided—after talking to the Goddess—that I no longer chose to be the ruling Prince. I realized I wanted to be selfish and choose my own final destiny.

"The poison that the traitor had given me over these past months has taken a lot of years off my normally long lifespan. Chances are I won't live many more decades. At least, not long enough to rule and do the things that must be done in order to unite all the wolf shifter clans the world over.

"The future is critical, Tara. The shifter clans must all come together under their one ruler, each one, and then learn to fight side by side. A war is coming. A battle that will rival all others. And those humans that are evil and determined to make us crawl under their rule just may triumph over us.

"The Goddess and I spoke of this future for a long time. I finally decided to give up my destined place and let my brother Colin rule in my stead. He is younger and stronger. He will lead us like no other before him."

Tara couldn't believe what she was hearing. What did this mean for her now? Her voice was shaky when she managed to ask, "What are you saying, exactly, Damian?" She shook her head in confusion. "You want me to marry Colin now?"

Damian sat back down on the bed beside her. "No, dear one. Colin has found his true-destined mate in your sister, Mara. The Goddess has decreed that the two of them shall rule." He smiled tenderly. "You are free, Tara. I give you complete freedom and you can go back to the one you love. I'm only sorry that all this had to happen, and so many were hurt, before it was all settled. Thanks to Logan we can rest in peace for awhile."

"Logan." His name sounded like a heart broken cry from her mouth. Damian raised his brows in question.

"I thought so."

Tara knew she was blushing—the heat spread over her. "What?"

"It's Logan you are in love with."

She couldn't deny it, didn't even want to anymore. But it wouldn't change anything. He didn't love her. "Yes. I'm sorry, Damian. I never meant for you to know or to be hurt by this. I'm still willing to marry you if that's what you want. Even though Colin and Mara will rule, I can still be by your side and help when needed."

"That, my dear sweet child, is why the Goddess has given us both this reprieve, this choice, this free will. Your selflessness is remarkable."

"I'm still not sure I understand what you're saying."

"Tara, I'm in love with someone else, too. We can all be free to be with the ones that our souls have chosen. You can go back to Logan." Damian chuckled again. "Although there was a time when I wouldn't have wished even my enemy to fall in love with that rogue cat, he's definitely a worthy man. He has proven himself time and again. He will make a daunting enemy to those who defy him and a strong ruler over his clans. I admire him, and I appreciate him." He grinned wolfishly at her. "And I even envy him a little. You will be the perfect mate."

Tara's heart sang. Was this real? Was she free? "I'm not dreaming, am I?"

Damian laughed. "I'd pinch you to prove you're awake but I have the feeling that if I left any mark on you—albeit small—then I'd have Logan to contend with."

Tara lowered her gaze. "He doesn't care." Those words nearly killed her.

"Hmm." Damian stood up. "I guess cat shifters show their feelings in a different way than wolf shifters do."

"Damian, do you like keeping me confused? Does this woman you love know this bad habit of yours?"

"You are an adorable little human. Lucky for me, Emily has the patience of the proverbial saint."

"Ah, Emily. That explains that."

"Yeah, I heard that she hovered over me the whole time. Kind of obvious, huh."

"She is a very nice woman." Tara smiled at him. "I liked her immediately."

"We have been in love all our lives," Damian admitted.

Tara was happy for them. She hoped Mara would be happy with Colin. "Perfect. Everyone gets a happy ending. Except me."

She didn't realize she'd spoken the words aloud until Damian chuckled yet again. "I don't know what to do now. It's hard to believe that after everything I've been through I'm actually free. Where will I go?"

"Ever been to Spokane?"

She shook her head at the odd question. "No."

"Well, at least there you won't have to live in a cave like you would have here. I hear that the penthouse is huge."

"Penthouse? I give up. I don't like talking to you."

"Logan's penthouse, sweetheart."

"What has that got to do with anything?" She asked the words with an aggravated growl in her voice. *Wow, that sounded authentic. I was obviously around Logan too long.*

"Why don't you ask him, yourself?"

"He left."

"He didn't go far," Damian smiled broadly. "He came back that night. He challenged me for the right to claim you as mate."

"What? Damian, I think my heart is beating too loud and I didn't hear you correctly."

"You heard right. He challenged me. He told me he was going to take you from me, and if that meant killing me and my entire pack he would do it."

Okay, that proved it. She really was dreaming! She was still unconscious and dreaming a happy ending to the nightmare that had plagued her every waking hour for years now.

She cleared her throat. "What happened? Did you fight him?"

"No. I told him that we would wait until you woke and let you make the decision. He wasn't happy about that, but he finally calmed down enough to agree."

"Where is he now?"

Damian stood up and walked to the door of the cave. Just as he started to answer, Logan walked in.

"I'm here."

Tara never saw the smile that passed between the two men. All she could concentrate on was Logan. He was really there! Their gazes locked from across the small space.

She finally broke the silence between them. "Is what Damian said true?"

"That I challenged him for you? Yeah."

"Is that all you're going to say?" She got off the bed and advanced on him. "Where does this leave us, Logan?"

"Together. Forever. If ... that's what you want."

She was shaking so hard she almost didn't make it across the room. She stumbled into his outstretched arms. He grabbed her up in his strong arms and lifted her high against his chest. He held her tight. "Are you sure, Logan?"

"Are you?" He searched her face. "I'm a shifter, Tara. I know how you feel about that."

"No, you don't." She caressed his lips with a soft touch. "It was never the fact that Damian was a shifter that bothered me. It was that I had no choice. I wanted to be loved. I wanted to fall in love. I didn't want to be forced to spend my life with a man I didn't love."

"Do you love me, angel?"

"Yes. I love you, Logan. With all my heart. With all my soul."

"Will you spend the rest of your life with me, as my mate, my love, my Queen?"

"Yes, yes, yes!"

"Good. I didn't relish the thought of having to fight every wolf here but I would if they tried to stop me from taking you home. Damian said he would let you choose, and they will honor that."

"Logan?"

"Yes, angel?"

"Do you love me?"

"More than life itself. Will you promise me something?"

"Anything."

"That could be interesting," he murmured teasingly, and then continued, "Promise me you will never again risk your life for anyone. I don't care who it is. Never again, Tara. I couldn't bear the thought of losing you."

"I can't promise that." She leaned in and kissed his lips lightly. "But I can promise that I will be more careful in how and when I use my healing powers. How's that?"

"You're going to be the death of me," he muttered. "I think I'm going to have to teach you what it means to be the mate of a cat shifter. Obedience plays a major role."

"Ha. You wish."

He kissed her. Tenderly. Long. "No. My wishing days are over. The only thing I could want is now in my arms."

"Don't ever let me go," she pleaded softly.

He grinned. "Angel, the day I kidnapped you was the day I knew you were mine forever. It just took me awhile to admit it to myself. My honor wouldn't let me claim you."

"Are you sure you want a half-human Goddess to rule by your side?" Tara searched his eyes. They shone with an blue glow that was mesmerizing. Her heart sang with joy.

Logan carried her back to the bed, laid her down in its center, and came down on top of her. He kissed her softly, gently, and Tara could feel his obvious restraint. "Oh, yeah, I'm more than sure," he murmured against her lips.

"Logan," Tara giggled and turned her face away to avoid his roaming lips. "We can't do this here. This is Damian's cave."

Logan growled and lovingly nipped her chin with his teeth. "He may be a wolf, but he's smart enough to know not to barge in. I'm sure he knows just what I had in mind the minute I knew you were finally awake."

"Oh?" Tara stared up into his face with all the love she could express in her gaze. "What exactly did you—do you—have in mind?"

"Sealing my claim. Claiming you ... heart ... body ... soul."

His lips touched hers. Their souls reached out to touch the other.

The Claim was complete.

• • •

Kari Thomas

Kari Thomas has been writing for years. An active member of RWA's Desert Rose and Northern Arizona chapters, this multi-published author is a bookaholic with over 3,000 titles in her collection. She loves to research subjects like history, religions and the supernatural. Raised in Florida, Thomas moved to Arizona in her teen years, and still resides there.

Printed in the United States
117201LV00001B/129/P